"I HAD A REALLY SMA[...] grade," Joe admitted[...]

"What happened in the third grade?" Annie asked.

"I met Mrs. Lacy. She was two years past retirement, stood four feet, two inches tall, and had a mean left hook. After a couple of rounds with some boxing gloves, we came to an understanding."

"Oh, so you made your mouth behave to please her?"

Joe grinned. "No, I discovered the girls don't like a smart mouth either. Speaking of mouths, yours has a tiny little pucker at the corner. Did you know that?"

He had gone all day not touching her and couldn't stand it a moment longer. He ran his finger across the top of her lips, teasing the corner as he studied it intently. By the time she realized he was about to do more, his lips were almost within kissing distance.

"No, Joe," she whispered, trying to control her trembling. "You promised."

"Ah, yes, I did," he murmured. "I got rid of my smart talk, Annie, but my mouth still has a mind of its own. . . ."

WHAT ARE *LOVESWEPT* ROMANCES?

They are stories of true romance and touching emotion. We believe those two very important ingredients are constants in our highly sensual and very believable stories in the LOVE-SWEPT line. Our goal is to give you, the reader, stories of consistently high quality that may sometimes make you laugh, sometimes make you cry, but are always fresh and creative and contain many delightful surprises within their pages.

Most romance fans read an enormous number of books. Those they truly love, they keep. Others may be traded with friends and soon forgotten. We hope that each LOVESWEPT romance will be a treasure—a "keeper." We will always try to publish

LOVE STORIES YOU'LL NEVER FORGET
BY AUTHORS YOU'LL ALWAYS REMEMBER

The Editors

Loveswept ® 758

Mac's Angels:
MIDNIGHT
FANTASY

SANDRA
CHASTAIN

BANTAM BOOKS
NEW YORK · TORONTO · LONDON · SYDNEY · AUCKLAND

MAC'S ANGELS: MIDNIGHT FANTASY
A Bantam Book / October 1995

If you would be interested in receiving protective vinyl covers for your
Loveswept books, please write to this address for information:

Loveswept
Bantam Books
P.O. Box 985
Hicksville, NY 11802

ISBN 0-553-44444-1

Published simultaneously in the United States and Canada

PRINTED IN THE UNITED STATES OF AMERICA

OPM   0 9 8 7 6 5 4 3 2 1

For Carol Springston, who gave me
her goose story and much more.

AUTHOR'S NOTE

At the Moonlight and Magnolias Writers' Conference in Atlanta last September, I heard a wonderfully uplifting story about geese. According to the speaker who relayed it, the author is unknown. It brought tears to my eyes, and I knew that I wanted to share it with you. For the purposes of this novel I have tried to paraphrase the story and modify it slightly. And if the writer is out there somewhere, please forgive any artistic license I've taken.

TOGETHER

In the fall, when you see geese heading south for the winter, flying along in a V formation, you see, not the reason for the V, only the beauty of their flight.

As each bird flaps its wings it creates an uplift for the bird immediately following. By flying in formation, the flock adds greater range than if each bird flew on its own.

Two people who share a common direction and need can get where they are going more quickly and easily because they are traveling on the thrust of each other.

When a goose falls out of formation, it suddenly feels the struggle of going alone . . . and quickly gets back into the V.

If we have the sense of a goose, we will stay in formation with those who are headed the same way we are.

When the leader gets tired, it rotates back in the wing and another goose flies point.

It is sensible to take turns, sharing the trip . . . with people or with geese flying south.

Geese honk from behind to encourage those up front to keep up their speed.

People who care about each other talk out their problems and reassure one another.

Finally, when a goose gets sick or is wounded and falls out of formation, its mate or another goose will follow it down to lend help and protection. The mate will stay with the fallen goose until it is able to fly or it dies.

If we have the sense of a goose, we will care about each other that way.

—ANONYMOUS

PROLOGUE

"Joe Armstrong, the all-American boy, is on self-destruct, Annie. I'm depending on you to turn him around and get him moving on the right track."

"But Mac, I know nothing about professional athletes. How do I reach him?"

"You knew nothing about housewives or teenagers either, and you handled them—not exactly as I would have preferred, but the end result was satisfactory; they rejoined the human race. I'm counting on you, Annie. Everything up to now has been practice. Consider this as your final exam."

Annie hung up the phone and let out a sigh. Mac had a way of making a person do what he wanted, whether you were confident with the assignment or not. She opened the folder again and studied her man.

Joe Armstrong was wealthy, drop-dead good-looking, single, and if their report was right, ready to end his life.

It was up to Annabelle Calloway to stop him, just like someone had once stopped her.

But how? How could she help a man who practically oozed sexuality when she could no longer tolerate a man's touch? How could she bring him back to life, when deep inside she was still dead?

Elsewhere, in the mountaintop headquarters known as Shangrila, Lincoln McAllister was holding another folder, a folder marked *Annabelle Calloway*. He hoped that he was doing the right thing in sending Annie to Joe.

If he was wrong, he'd lose them both.

ONE

Joe Armstrong sloshed the last swallow of Scotch around in his glass and grimaced. When had he started drinking Scotch? he wondered. As a college student and in his early years as a football player, he hadn't drunk at all.

Joe Armstrong, the son of the Reverend and Mrs. Jacob Armstrong of Eufaula, Alabama; the boy who became the darling of the sports world; the player who led the fumbling Atlanta Falcons to the Super Bowl for the first time in history—that Joe Armstrong hadn't touched a drop. But he wasn't that guy anymore—not since the accidents.

Joe shrugged his shoulders and let his eyes drift over to the television set, where a popular late-night host was switching back and forth between his California studio and the crowd gathering in Times Square. The scene seemed as cold and flat as Joe's mood.

The ring of the telephone cut through the silence. Joe didn't move. He listened as the answering machine cut in with his standard message, "It's your quarter, start talking."

The caller was Ace, another of the endless chain of old teammates who'd become casual acquaintances in the last months. "Where are you, Joe? Time's a-passing. You're going to miss ringing in the New Year. Get your blankety-blank ass over here."

The message was recorded, and instantly filed away with the other callers who'd invited him to celebrate the New Year. Joe hadn't responded. What was there to celebrate? The last thing he wanted in his life was a new year to screw up. His friends wouldn't appreciate his frame of mind. They'd be better off without him.

He lifted the glass and swallowed his drink, then grimaced and struggled to his feet. The evidence of his holiday hell lay all around the condo. A sad little Christmas tree, sent over by some woman who was unable to give up her hope of reviving a dying relationship, leaned against the wall in the corner. He hadn't even plugged it in, forgetting about it unless the weight of his steps set off the sleigh bells that served as its primary decorations.

Empty pizza boxes, beer bottles, and square little white boxes that once contained Chinese food dotted the table and floor like dilapidated tombstones in an old cemetery.

Cemetery. Joe was back to thoughts of death again.

Death. The first time he'd met death had been when his parents had died. The loss had almost killed him. When his pal Jack died, he wished it had.

Joe closed his eyes and opened them again. Of late he hadn't been able to drum up even a little emotion. Other than Rob, his agent, the man at the liquor store, and the fast-food deliverymen, he hadn't spoken to anyone he knew personally for weeks. He felt like a character in a movie he'd seen who had been condemned to live one single day of his life over and over again.

Stumbling to the window, Joe looked out, expecting any minute to see the Ghost of Christmas Past glide through the glass and zap him back in time.

"No way, Armstrong," he groused. "You can't go back. You had your chance and you blew it." As always, the haze of the alcohol seemed to evaporate much too soon. He was certainly too sober to expect a diapered, bright-eyed babe in a top hat to appear. The only guest he'd get was the old man in flowing robes with a long beard.

What the hell? What was the point of prolonging the inevitable? At the time when he'd expected to provide for his father and mother, who'd worked all their lives to see that he got what he needed, they weren't there to be provided for. At the time when he expected to be at the zenith of his career, his career was fading. At the time when he'd normally be celebrating with Jack, there was no Jack.

Even Rob was beginning to lose patience. Image, Rob had explained, was all Joe had to market, and his career was alive only as long as his name stayed in the public eye. But Joe wasn't comfortable hawking products and he didn't have the quick wit and inflated opinion of himself necessary to do broadcasting.

His ability was suspect, and he wasn't sure he wanted any part of coaching. That would mean taking responsibility for other men. Joe Armstrong was definitely not strong on responsibility, not even on his own team.

A sprained knee had taken him out of the game over a month ago, and in spite of prodding by the coach and the trainer to return to practice, Joe hadn't even dressed out for the last two weeks.

At thirty-six, Joe Armstrong was a football quarterback whose arm and knees were gone. A ballplayer whose heart had been chiseled away a sliver at a time. He didn't know how to do anything else. He had nothing left to give, and tonight he was through pretending. He didn't deserve to be the one still alive.

Maybe he'd go for a long drive, find a bridge, and become the James Stewart of the nineties. He didn't believe in angels and he no longer looked forward to a "wonderful life."

If Joe Armstrong disappeared off the face of the earth, who'd miss him?

The stark truth was—nobody.

Joe lifted the glass once more, then realized it was empty. The low sound of the partygoers on the television set suddenly rose. The apple at the top of the tower at Times Square had begun its descent. For a moment Joe watched it, every click signaling the last dying moments of a miserable year.

"Thirty seconds."

"Twenty seconds."

"Ten."

"Nine."

"Eight."

Joe took his keys from his pocket and lurched to the door, turning back one last time.

"Three."

"Two."

"One."

The apple reached the bottom.

Joe reached for the doorknob.

The crowd yelled.

The doorbell rang.

"What? Who the hell?" He jerked open the door. "Go away. I told you—"

The woman standing on his doorstep looked like one of the snowflakes from the *Nutcracker* ballet. No, with a mass of feathery golden hair nestled with a crown of jewels, she looked like an angel. She was wearing some kind of sassy, short gold dress, gold stockings, and gold shoes.

He must be hallucinating.

"You haven't left yet," she said in relief. "I

didn't expect snow, and I was afraid I might miss you."

Joe closed his eyes and opened them again. "Snow?"

"Yep. It started about an hour ago. I should have allowed for the unexpected, but I thought you'd appreciate my arrival more if I looked glamorous and exciting, so I bought a new dress. What do you think?"

Joe didn't think. He couldn't. The ethereal creature with the impossibly long legs and high-heeled shoes had whirled around, moved past him, and turned back to smile at him once more.

"I must be dreaming," he said.

"You're not dreaming. I promise."

"You're real?"

"Do you want me to be?"

Somebody was playing a joke on him. His vision was beginning to cloud, and he didn't feel too steady on his feet. "I want you to explain yourself. No, cancel that. I want you to get out of here and leave me alone. I was about to—"

"I know. You were about to do what you didn't do before—end it all. Find a curve at the top of a slick road and just drive off into tomorrow. Close the door. I didn't want to mess up the image I was going for by wearing a jacket, and I didn't have one that would match. Now I'm turning into an icicle."

Joe closed the door and leaned heavily against it. "Who *are* you?"

She could have told him that she was Annabelle

Calloway, but that wouldn't have meant anything to him. Besides, in this case, it wasn't who she was but what she was there for that counted, and she might as well get started on explaining that.

"Does it matter? You've been sitting here all night wishing you had someone to care about you. Now you do—me." She glanced around. "Just look at this place. Good heavens." She paused, then laughed lightly. "I can't believe I said that, but then I guess there's nothing good about hell, is there?"

Heaven or hell, he didn't really care. At least this figment of his imagination was a new twist on the nightmares that he'd been having. It was a damned sight better than accidents and pain. He might as well see where the hallucination went. "Okay, I'll play along. Who sent you?"

"Does it matter?"

"I mean are you some kind of 'angelgram'? Where are your wings?"

"I've been called an angel. But I prefer to call myself a kind of retriever."

Joe laughed in disbelief. "The only retriever I know is a dog who belongs to a friend, and it's in the kennel for the holidays."

She only smiled. She'd allow him to work out his questions in his own way. Considering her past fiascoes, being seen as a dog was better than being an angel.

"I need another drink," Joe said, and lurched back to the art-deco bar some decorator had thought appropriate for a playboy jock.

She knew that liquor wouldn't help. He'd already gone as far down that road as he could go. "No more booze, big guy. The only thing you're going to get tonight is food." She wrinkled her nose. "And a bath. In fact, I think we'll reverse the order. Bath first."

Her entrance might have been intriguing, but now she was becoming too bossy. "And who appointed you my keeper?" Joe growled, his head beneath the countertop as he threw empty bottles behind him like a dog digging a hole to bury his bone.

"I don't think you'd understand if I told you. At least not yet." She walked over to the man who, when standing, would tower over her, and put her hand on his shoulder. "Joe."

A spasm of heat shot through him as if he'd been jolted with a laser beam. For a moment he couldn't even move. Then he turned his head and looked straight into the stern frown of his fantasy warden.

"I said a bath first, Joe. Do you want to take it by youself, or shall I help you?"

The crown of snowflakes in her hair had melted, leaving droplets of water that caught and reflected the light from the bar. Like a kaleidoscope, her face seemed refracted in swirls of color and light. Joe had seen a lot of things that weren't there, but this particular figment was something he was having a hard time understanding. She seemed to be real, but he knew she couldn't be.

"A shower. A cold shower," he repeated, rising. "That's what I need. Then he'll come, the old man with the beard. I can deal with him. Golden Girl has to go."

"Old man with a beard?"

He nodded. If his hallucination wanted to chat, hey, he was cool. "Sure. I can deal with him. Just let that baby wearing the top hat go on the Leno show. Send me the old guy."

"Oh, you mean Father Time."

His golden girl smiled and followed him up the stairs, picking up the clothing he discarded as he walked. "Sorry," she said. "I'm not old and I don't have a beard."

She was right about that. "Fine"—he continued the game—"but if you want to be the baby, you're going to have to take off those long legs and that angel dress. The baby only wears a diaper and a top hat."

"I don't think so, Joe." She stooped and added his T-shirt to the stack of clothing lying across her arm. "Then again, maybe I will get rid of the shoes." She slipped them off and placed them against the wall just inside his bedroom door.

"I knew it," he said gleefully as he turned and dropped his briefs. "She's shrinking, disappearing, and I haven't even seen her fly."

Seen her fly? She took one look at the totally nude man before her and felt any sound she might have made dry up and turn to cotton in her throat.

John Joseph Armstrong might be a wounded

warrior who'd been involved in a series of life-altering tragedies, but his body would have argued with that statement all the way into any woman's most erotic dream. Except for a multitude of scars, he was just about perfect. If *Playgirl* were looking for a centerfold, they'd move right past Bruce Willis and Mel Gibson and settle on Joe.

Annie realized why Mac had been so insistent on assigning her to Joe. Her boss was obviously looking for a way to test her ability to do her job and keep her objectivity, and he couldn't have come up with a better subject.

"What's wrong, Golden Girl, I don't hear a bell ringing. Even James Stewart heard a bell ring every time an angel saved a soul and got her wings. Has your dinger jammed?"

Dinger jammed?

He had a colorful, disarming way of expressing himself, but she suspected that it was all an act to cover up his lonely desperation. Once she'd been a pro at the same thing. It was ironic that he was remembering the famous old Christmas movie. Ironic because she'd watched that movie over and over the Christmas she'd reached her lowest point. She must have nodded, for Joe smiled in understanding.

Whatever the state of her dinger, his was operating just fine.

"Shower," she said. "Very cold shower."

"You too," he said. "If I'm going to sober up,

I'm not going to do it alone. You gotta get nekked, too."

"Absolutely not!"

He reached for his briefs. "Then neither do I."

"All right, big guy, close your eyes."

He could do that. It wasn't a bit hard. In fact, if he weren't careful, he'd close them until tomorrow, and that was the last thing he wanted to do. He'd seen demons who wouldn't survive in the light of day, but he'd never had such a sensual hallucination, and he wasn't ready to give her up. He could always put off his plans for a midnight ride until another night.

With what he knew must be a stupid grin, he closed his eyes, grabbing at the doorframe to hold himself upright when the room began to swim. "I'm going to count to three, so you'd better be quick."

He never got to two. Her hand on the site of his last shoulder injury turned him toward the bathroom with no argument. The shower water was ice-cold, followed by steaming hot, then cold again. By the time he was prune-shrunk and shivering, his eyes seemed to have refocused themselves, and he opened the shower door.

There was no one there. Only the leg of his jeans hanging from the clothes hamper suggested that anyone had been in the room.

"Damn, Joe, you really did it this time. You found heaven and lost it. So what's new about that? You'd probably screw up hell." He reached for the towel and decided that those jewels he'd imagined in his tormentor's hair had jumped ship and turned into ice picks that were attacking his scalp.

Too bad he'd stepped into that shower. He was beginning to like his angelic tormentor. If Scotch whisky could conjure her up again, he might order another case.

Wrapping the towel around his waist, he stumbled to the bed and fell across it. Moments later he was asleep, his inner self desperately seeking the woman who'd come to his door. What he found instead was Father Time, and the old man was holding out his hand.

In the kitchen, Annie Calloway was standing in front of the refrigerator studying the decaying remains of what once must have been food. No wonder the rest of the house was filled with take-out containers. She just wondered how Joe Armstrong had gotten anybody to deliver to such a remote area.

She wondered how Mac's driver had found the narrow A-frame on the side of the north Atlanta hill.

She wondered again why Mac had decided to send her there. How he chose his subjects for "repatriation" was one subject he never discussed. Where he got the money to operate a rescue business that was definitely nonprofit was just as much a mystery. But his staff accepted his conditions and zealously protected his insistence on total anonymity. He worked exclusively from the mountaintop retreat he referred to as Shangrila, and communicated only by phone.

Annie gave the gold spandex skirt a tug and wished she'd worn something more practical. Knocking Joe's socks off had seemed important when she was choosing her wardrobe. She'd done that all right.

Now it was time to put away her angel dress and don her working clothes. She had an assignment to do and only six days to do it. Joe Armstrong didn't know it, but it was payback time, and he was her last chance.

She glanced at the clock. Day one of her six was under way. She'd better get moving. What a way to start a new year, cleaning up behind a drunk who looked like a Greek god and lived in a half-furnished house with a bar, a couch, and a Christmas tree decorated with sleigh bells.

A quick check through the window told her that she wasn't going to dash out to the road and retrieve the bags she'd left by the mailbox. For the time being she'd have to borrow something from Joe.

Moving to the bedroom, she leaned her ear against the door and listened until she heard the unmistakable sound of snoring. Quietly she opened the door and tiptoed to Joe's bureau, where she found a drawer filled with T-shirts. She pulled one shirt out and backed out of the room, resolutely keeping her attention on the floor.

When she heard a hiccuping noise and the sound of movement, she looked without thinking. He hadn't awakened, but he had lost his towel.

The light from the hall spilled through the open door, casting a golden glow across his nude body. He was lying on his stomach, his face framed by one arm. There was a light shadow of beard on his chin that was a shade darker than his ash-colored hair. Warrior, yes. He could have been a Viking, she decided, home from a night of raiding and pillaging. All he needed was a bearskin coverlet and a maiden.

Whoa, Annabelle! This is a fantasy for Joe, not you. Carefully she pulled the blanket from the foot of the bed and covered him, caught for a moment by the gentleness of his features when he was relaxed in sleep. It was too bad that Joe had lost his throwing arm. He seemed to have simply given up. Other athletes played longer. Other athletes had plans for a life after football.

Joe had neither.

She had to find a way to make him believe in himself again.

TWO

Joe swam through the thick cottony haze of sleep one layer at a time.

"You can do this," he said with a groan, moving one hand slowly up his nude body to grab the top of his head before it took a rocket blast into outer space.

"On the other hand," he mumbled, letting his hand fall to the pillow beside his head, "why would you want to?"

"Because, you either get up and come to the kitchen for black coffee, or I will insert a stomach tube and force-feed you. Your choice, Bucko."

One of Alvin's chipmunks had escaped and was chirping annoyingly in his ear. He swatted at the creature. "Go away!"

"No way, José! Open your eyes. Look outside. The sun is shining. Everything is covered in snow, and it looks like fairyland."

A stream of light so bright that it penetrated closed eyelids hit him in the face. He made an attempt to turn over, groaned, and again reached for the top of his head, hoping to hold it in place.

"I don't know who you are or what you think you're doing," he growled as he managed to rise up and cock one eye, "but I'll give you about two seconds to disappear."

"Golden Girl, I think, is what you decided to call me last night. Like I said, it's your choice. I've been called lots of things. Let me help you."

She lifted the sheet and caught both his ankles, jerking his feet off the bed and allowing them to fall to the floor with a thump. "Now you're halfway there. Want to give me your hands?"

Wait a minute. Golden Girl—Golden. Something was coming back. A hallucination, a different kind of imaginary nighttime demon, a fantasy angel, wearing wings—no, wearing a pair of lacy gold stockings and high-heeled shoes . . .

Joe managed to get one eye fully open and focused. He hadn't been dreaming. She was there, hands on hips, golden-blond hair shining like an angel's in a Renaissance painting. He blinked, opening both eyes this time.

She was definitely there. Except this time she wasn't wearing fairy clothes or angel wings. She was wearing a pink jogging suit and running shoes.

"Is this some kind of joke? Who sent you?"

"It's no joke, and it doesn't matter who sent me, only that I'm here."

Slowly, in spite of the attack of the ice picks in his brain, he forced his protesting body to sit up. "Okay. So we both agree that you're here. The next question is why?"

"Now that's a question I've been giving considerable thought to. Why anybody would think you're worth salvaging is beyond me."

He allowed his eyes to focus on the room, trying to avoid the stream of light that still threatened to blind him if he faced it head-on. Moving his fingers carefully, one at a time, he tested his reflexes. He felt as if he was awake, though sometimes his feelings the morning after a binge were misleading.

He tried his toes. They responded to his mental commands, registering the soft thick texture of the carpet. The sensation of touch was there, and he'd lost it often enough during his years on the ball field to know that he could actually walk on feet that didn't feel anything at all.

Gingerly continuing his physical assessment, he touched his head. He already knew that it was an exploding minefield. Moving his fingertips downward, he reached the mass of wiry hair that covered his chest. No pain about the rib cage. Good.

His stomach rumbled in protest, though it was difficult just yet to be sure whether it was asking or refusing an as-yet-unvoiced request for food. More body hair—

"Great balls of fire!" He stood up. "What have you done to me?"

"I? Done to you?" The amused feminine voice repeated. "As in have my way with your body?" She gave a strained laugh. "Don't worry, Joe. Your virtue is intact."

This time his eyes opened, viewed, and closed again in acute embarrassment. He wasn't wearing a stitch. He was with a beautiful woman whom he only barely remembered, and his masculinity was as used up and limp as his career.

"Would you like me to dress you?" she asked. "The coffee is ready, but I need you to come to the kitchen to drink it. You showered last night, but you can do so again if it will help."

What he was seeing and hearing was making less and less sense. One thing was clear: another shower was in order. At least it was private, and the cold water would be an excuse for the pitiful state of his body in the presence of a golden goddess.

"Fine! A shower first." He started to pull the sheet from the bed, then dropped it and strode into the bathroom with as much dignity as he could muster. What difference did it make now? Modesty had vanished sometime in the wee hours of the morning, after that damned apple dropped and the spaceship wielding that tractor beam of magnetic light had locked onto his bed.

Ten minutes later, after cold water had restored some degree of rationality to his befuddled brain, he dried himself, brushed his teeth, then pulled on a pair of soft blue sweatpants that were hanging on the back of the bathroom door. Carefully he opened the door and stepped out.

The room was vacant. Maybe he'd just experienced a flashback, he thought, the kind Vietnam vets had, that drinkers experienced when they'd finally gone too far. Then he caught sight of the bed, all neatly made, the pillows fluffed and covered by the spread. It hadn't looked like that since the day that flaky decorator had given him a personal tour.

As a matter of fact, if he remembered correctly, it hadn't looked like that for more than five minutes, once she'd offered him a sample of her nondecorating expertise. He'd refused, but her vigorous invitation had left the bed mussed, and it had rarely been made again.

Until now.

Joe Armstrong, the first quarterback to lead the once hapless Atlanta Falcon football team to a Super Bowl championship, was suddenly cold sober and scared silly. No matter how many times he'd had too much to drink, he'd never conjured up this kind of morning after.

He ran his fingers through still-damp hair, pulled on a T-shirt that was wrinkled but still reasonably clean, and found the last matching pair of athletic socks in the drawer. His shoes were missing, but at least his feet were warm as he left the bedroom and started down the stairs.

At the bottom he studied the great room in disbelief. He remembered enough about the previous night to know that he'd left the area in a state of disaster. Now there were no bottles, no cans, no empty pizza boxes, and no newspapers. The television was turned off, probably for the first time in weeks, and the smell of coffee wafted through the door from the tiny kitchen.

In the kitchen, Annie Calloway stood listening. She'd heard the big football player moving slowly around the room above her. She hoped he was dressing. Soon he'd see the results of her whirlwind cleaning spree.

Though she'd offered him coffee, it was lunchtime and the meal she'd prepared was more in the nature of a cleansing of the system. Coffee, dry toast, which made practical use of the bread she'd found, and clear soup. Once he was completely sober, she'd have to tell him why she was there. Of course, confessing was optional. Her assignments gave her a great deal of latitude in handling explanations of herself and her reasons for being where she was.

Once she'd pretended to be someone's surprise birthday gift. Another time she'd acted as a housekeeper. She'd even been a long-lost cousin who needed a place to stay and someone to give *her* a hand. Her stories varied, but the end results were expected to be the same: reclaim the lost and plant their feet on the path to a better life.

"Damn!" she whispered. That sounded sanctimonious. Anybody who knew her knew how totally out of character that was. Annie Calloway, once known as the soap-opera star Annice, was on probation herself for her unorthodox methods and her questionable successes. Granted, her first project—a mother who'd been ready to run away with her gardener—had decided that life with her banker husband was more secure, but Annie couldn't entirely claim the credit. Once the poor woman had a few days of firsthand experience living in the gardener's quarters after a strange odor had forced her out of her house, she'd decided that her husband wasn't as dull as she'd thought.

There also had been the young motorcyclist who'd thought he'd died, gone to heaven, and been rescued by an angel. From the time he recovered from his head wounds and regained his eyesight, he'd decided that the hereafter was a great deal better than the present, and he clung to Annie, first as his savior, then, to her surprise, as the woman he wanted in his bed. She'd thought he was still a child. She'd been wrong.

Annie had hoped the attractive young therapist she'd arranged to stop by his room would hasten his recovery, if not his sexual education. Only because the boy had been physically unable to do more than have vivid dreams of a personal relationship had she been saved from disaster.

After a strong reprimand from her superior for not sticking to proper procedure, she'd been reminded that she had to carry out her work without personal involvement. She was a professional, or she would be once she passed her probation, and she was to act accordingly. There was to be absolutely no more touchy-feely, or she'd get the boot!

But Mac hadn't seen Joe Armstrong nude.

She looked up as Joe appeared in the doorway. Mac hadn't seen Joe clothed either. Annie shivered, turned, and upset the sugar bowl, spraying a path of white crystals across the red tiled floor from his bare feet to hers.

"You're real?" His voice was deep and gravelly.

"Come and sit down. I'll pour the coffee."

"Thanks, but I'll take a beer."

"I don't think so." She lifted the dustpan from its nail on the side of the cabinet and reached for the broom. "I emptied all the cans."

He growled and started toward the refrigerator, sliding on the sugar crystals in his stocking feet like a child playing on an icy lake. He plowed straight into his pint-sized drill sergeant, sending the dustpan in one direction and the broom in the other. Before he could right himself, he'd knocked her feet from beneath her and she was lying on top of his body in the middle of his kitchen floor.

This time he didn't have to apologize for his lack of response. His body didn't fail him. He couldn't have stopped it if he'd tried.

"Is this in the nature of a 'slam, bam, thank you, ma'am' hello?" she asked, trying to control a shaky voice that was much too shrill. It took every ounce of her control to remain still. *He isn't going to hurt* you, Annie. This was a simple accident. It could have happened to anyone. Besides—it was your fault.*

Moments passed as Joe felt the return of the ice picks in his head. "Well, it's a beginning," was as snappy a reply as Joe could manage, considering he'd cracked the back of his head on the Mexican-tile floor.

"Get up, you big lug!" his captive began, trying to disentangle herself from his grasp.

"Not so fast, Golden Girl. Time out. I seem to have lost my game plan here. Was I injured last night and don't remember bringing you home?"

"Injured? No. You didn't bring me home. I brought myself, and technically it was midnight when I rang the bell. But by the time I got inside, the apple had already fallen and it was the beginning of a new year."

"The apple. I remember. It fell and the doorbell rang. I opened it, and there you were, standing there like some kind of angel in the snow. You were wearing a crown."

"No, my hair was covered with snow."

"It melted and the water turned into diamonds." His voice was gentler, soothing, as if he were a caregiver and she a child in need. "They match the flecks in your eyes. What color are they—green? I never saw eyes exactly this color before. And your lips—they're—"

"No. Stop." With a sudden sinking feeling, Annie realized that she was holding his massive shoulders instead of pushing away. A little tickle in the back of her throat felt suspiciously like the beginning of a sob.

He didn't argue. Instead, his fingertips gently traced the curve of her eyebrow as if he'd never examined one up close. Carrying on the easy banter had been fun, but he was building a sense of togetherness and she couldn't let that happen. Anxiety had already set in.

"Please," she whispered, frantic now to put distance between them.

"All right. If you're sure."

If only she weren't so afraid. She could see a scar on his face from injuries administered long ago. Once, in some past time, he'd had his nose broken. It had healed, but where its length had once been aquiline and proud, it now announced its hard-earned toughness to the world. He had a strong, not-yet-defeated look that dared her to challenge his authority.

She didn't.

"I'm going to get up now, Joe," she said quietly.

"Why? I rather like this. I've explored the floor of my kitchen before, but never so intimately or so sweetly." He flicked a sugar crystal from her chin and pressed it to his tongue, where it dissolved. He swallowed with open appreciation.

She rolled off him and, amid the crunch of sugar, allowed her uncertainty to vent itself. "I'll just bet you have, Bucko. From the looks of this place, you must pass out regularly in front of the refrigerator."

He smiled. "Oh? How can you tell?"

"Because it was the only clean spot on the floor before I mopped it. Get up, Joe."

Joe came lazily to his feet, a smile planted across his face, brushing first his bottom, then his socks with his hands. "Give me the broom. I'll sweep."

"Are you sure you know how?"

"I know how to do a lot of things, Goldy, I just don't always do them."

Moments later Joe found himself outside the kitchen door emptying the crystals into the trash. He glanced at the snow-covered landscape and let a gasp of surprise escape his lips.

"It's very beautiful," Annie said, coming to stand beside him.

He took a long look at her. "It sure is." It wasn't the low-hanging branches heavy with snow that he was referring to. "Did I really call you Golden Girl?"

"That's what you said."

"Odd, I don't remember."

"Well, it might have been because of the dress I was wearing. Or it might have been because I told you I was a retriever of lost souls."

He remembered that dress all right, but the rest . . . "A retriever?"

"You said the only retriever you knew was your friend's dog, and she was in the kennel."

"He. My friend's the she."

"Sorry, he." Annie shivered and stepped back. It wasn't entirely the cold that directed her move,

but she blocked the thought away and began to re-
fill the sugar bowl. "Come and eat."

"Eating isn't exactly what's on my mind now,
Goldy. As a matter of fact, I'm reasonably certain
that eating isn't even a smart move. You understand
I'm speaking from past experience. The day after a
big New Year's Eve celebration isn't the best time
for ham and eggs."

"Your celebration was pitifully small, and there
is no ham. Only dry toast and black coffee. Come
and sit down."

Joe found himself following her directions, fas-
cinated that a woman barely five feet six inches tall
thought herself capable of harassing a two-
hundred-pound football player.

When she placed the coffee and saucer with two
pieces of browned bread before him, he looked at
her in amusement. "You're serious? Toast and black
coffee?"

"I'm serious. If you can handle that, you may
have a bowl of chicken soup."

"I have a headache and a hangover, not a case of
the flu."

She poured herself a cup of coffee and sat down
across the table from him. "Same treatment."

He didn't think so, but he didn't argue. "What
about some cream?"

"Cream probably isn't a good idea, given the
uncertain state of your stomach, Joe."

"My stomach is fine." He poured a generous
portion of the cream into his cup. A good move, for

the coffee was strong enough to walk out the back door unassisted. He took two swallows, then followed with a bite of cold toast. "What is this, your surefire cure-'em-or-kill-'em recipe?"

"Close enough."

Gamely he swallowed the first piece of toast, washing it down with huge gulps of the hot liquid. She could tell from the expression on his face, combined with a series of deep, quick swallows, that he wasn't going to be ready for the soup right away.

"According to the radio, the snow has started to melt. It will probably freeze again and turn into ice. All in all we're probably stuck here for the next two days."

"We?"

"We," she confirmed. "I told you, I've been assigned to get you shaped up, and I only have six days in which to do it. We'll spend today working out the game plan."

He might have questioned her more, except the coffee and the toast in his stomach were challenging the ice picks inside his skull. The cream-laden coffee was on the verge of giving up the fight when Joe stood and dashed back up the stairs, mercifully reaching the bathroom before he lost the race.

Half an hour later he reappeared, wearing wrinkled jeans, a T-shirt with the name of a heavy-metal band across the front, and a sheepish expression on his face.

"Was it my cooking?" she asked innocently as

she flipped the page in the scrapbook she was studying.

"No, it was my eating."

"Ready for the soup?"

"Not in this lifetime. I think I'll just have a nice cup of herbal tea."

She chuckled. "Herbal tea? The great Joe Armstrong drinks herbal tea?"

"Yeah. Don't tell a soul, will you? It would spoil the image I've tried diligently to create."

She turned another page. "Oh? What image is that, party animal of Atlanta?"

"No, stud of the South."

"Well, unless you're a medieval throwback, I'd say you got an early start on that, if this centerfold is any example."

Joe sat on the arm of the couch and leaned over her shoulder, inspecting her reading material. "What the . . . ? Where'd you find that?"

She was holding the photo album open to a full-page picture of Joe stretched out against a black bearskin rug, wearing nothing but a beaming smile. He bore no resemblance to the man she'd seen the night before. In the photo Joe was only six months old.

"It was right here, under the coffee table, along with some others. You've kept quite a record of your achievements."

"Not me," Joe admitted in a low voice, "it was my mother. She kept all these albums."

"She must have been very proud of your accomplishments—graduating from college, becoming a professional football player, winning the Super Bowl."

"I never graduated from college. Still lack fifteen hours. And she didn't get to see the Super Bowl. She and my father were killed in a car wreck the week before."

Annie didn't tell him that she already knew they were dead. "What did you major in?"

"Physical education and—you want a real laugh—counseling."

"I would think that's a perfect combination if you want to deal with young people. What's wrong with it?"

"You've got to be kidding. How many people would think I'm a good enough example to counsel a child?"

The silence that followed spoke louder than words to Annie. Joe had loved his parents very much and they'd been proud of him. Joe hadn't started to change until after their deaths, when the albums had ended.

It had been three years since the Falcons had won the Super Bowl. Three years before, Joe Armstrong had started his slide into oblivion—just about the time Annie Calloway had started to make her own exit.

Annie had been rescued from oblivion.

Joe had just kept sliding.

THREE

Annie closed the scrapbook and moved away from Joe.

"About that lunch, Joe?" She was having a hard time equating the bright-eyed expression of that child with the hollow one in the adult.

"About that beer you emptied," he retorted. "Surely you saved one. I think I need something to clear my head this morning."

That was a lie if he'd ever told one. His head was much too clear. What he wanted was to erase the sudden intrusion of his mother's presence. He didn't want to think about her. He'd become reasonably successful in not thinking about anything other than the present—until Golden Girl had intruded in his life, studying him with the same nononsense look his mother had used when she wanted to con him into facing up to his sins. Accomplishing that was no mean feat. Now he didn't just want a beer, he needed one, and he had no intention of letting a golden-haired drill sergeant whip him into shape.

She simply shook her head. "No more beer! No more alcohol of any kind, Joe. That's part of the new game plan. Do you understand?"

"No! I don't understand." He didn't. He didn't even know what she was doing in his house. Few women had seen the inside and none had been asked to stay. But there Goldy was, cleaning, sitting on his couch, cooking in his kitchen, giving every indication that she was there for the duration— whatever that was.

"Who are you?" he asked. "No more fun and games. I want the truth."

"I could tell you, Joe. I could tell you that I was sent by someone who understands what you're going through, someone who cares. But I don't think you'd understand. Not yet. Haven't you ever taken something or someone on faith?"

No, he couldn't recall that he had. And she was right, he didn't understand, but there was a strong voice inside his head that suggested his agent had had a hand in the matter. He'd warned Rob about interfering. Nobody understood what he was going through, and in spite of Rob's protests, the cold truth was, nobody cared.

"No. Faith means you have to believe in something or somebody. I don't."

Watching the set of his shoulders, Annie understood the burden he was carrying. "And that's why

I'm here, Joe," she said softly. "Your way didn't work. Now we're going to try my game plan."

He didn't want to admit she was right, and he didn't want to feel the faint flicker of need that she seemed determined to expose.

"What about it, Joe?"

"Just for the sake of argument, the only game I play now is Scrabble."

"I like Scrabble, but that isn't what I had in mind."

"Oh? Then what is your game plan, coach?"

"That's what we have to work out, starting with the rules."

Now that he could see her up close, without the intermediary of an alcoholic fog, he could truly appreciate the way her eyes sparkled, the softness of her skin in spite of the tiny lines that seemed to radiate from her right ear, gradually disappearing across her cheek. He'd seen enough scars in his day to recognize the remains of an injury, in spite of the masterful job some surgeon had done on her face.

He liked that about her. A thing shouldn't be too perfect. Impurities, even small ones, made a thing of beauty more precious. Even a woman. Scars were badges of courage, or, he admitted, foolishness. He wondered for a moment how she'd gotten hers.

"The rules, Joe," she snapped, deliberately drawing him back to the present. "We need to talk about them."

In that moment he stopped kidding himself.

She'd gotten to him. It hadn't taken her long to dissolve his plan to be tough, and it wasn't just her businesslike manner. He liked the saucy way she issued orders. If the Falcons' coach, June Jones, had hired an assistant like Goldy, it wouldn't have taken him so long to get the team moving in the right direction.

"Rules?" He gave her a disarming grin. "You mean like laws or curfews and fines?"

"I mean like goal setting, therapy, counseling, and motivational study."

The identity of her boss was becoming even more intriguing. It couldn't be anyone with the Falcons; they really didn't need him anymore. They had a younger quarterback who had the hottest arm in the league.

Joe hadn't wanted to hear it, but every sports-medicine doctor in the Southeast had already told him the truth; he was on the downhill side of his career. Not only had the fun gone out of his game but the expertise had as well.

"I see. And all this goal setting will make my knees run and my arm accurate? I don't think so."

"No. This game plan has nothing to do with your sports career, it's geared to making you a productive human being with a purpose."

He'd started out defeated. Now he seemed intent on covering up with a good-old-boy attitude. She wasn't sure she liked that attitude any better. It was just a different kind of escape.

"I have—excuse me—had a purpose in life, and

I fulfilled it. Now? Let's don't kid ourselves, sweet thing, I'm doing the only thing I can still do well. Nothing."

Annie wanted to smack him. "Stop that right now! I don't tolerate giving up."

He simply stared at her for a long minute, then gave a disbelieving laugh. "You don't tolerate— Listen, Goldy, I haven't been a productive citizen in a long time. It's too late to start over now."

"You could."

"No. You don't ever get over the guilt. Once I lost"—he swallowed back his admission that he'd lost his parents—"once I was replaced on the football field, the only purpose in my life got left behind."

"We'll find a new one."

Suddenly he was tired. His head hurt and his stomach was beginning to feel the kind of empty that makes you want to eat at the same time it's warning you not to.

"Let's cut the crap, Goldy, and get to the bottom line. If this is a joke, I'm not laughing."

"It isn't a joke, Joe."

"What then? If you're after my body, it's yours."

"I'm not after your body, not in the physical sense."

The weary artificial banter stopped, as did his anger, replaced with a kind of dead honesty. "Sorry, Goldy, if you want more, believe me, there isn't any. What you see is what you get. Anything else was used up a long time ago."

"I don't believe that for a minute. I know better."

"Oh? And who appointed you as the all-wise, all-knowing oracle to fallen heroes?"

Annie gulped. "I could tell you, but I don't think you're ready to hear it yet." She studied the man carefully. He'd had a night's sleep and another shower, but without a shave, he was still the wounded warrior.

Annie refused to believe that there was nothing beneath his surface. There had to be, or she wouldn't have been sent to help him. She wouldn't be responding to him on some level that she thought long gone. Her need to comfort him was spilling over into a need to be comforted in return.

"Look, Golden Girl, I've had almost every trick in the book played on me. I've had women wait in my car. They've talked maids into opening my hotel room, and one even posed as a police officer and pulled me over on the highway. But I've never had one move into my house set on becoming my nanny."

His observation was eerily accurate. She felt her face flush as she forced her attention back to her mission. "What did you do?"

He shook his head as if he were trying to focus on his answer. "What did I do about what?"

"All those women? I can't imagine that you said no to them. Just listen, Joe."

Her voice was soft and urgent, as if she had a lot to say and only a few seconds in which to say it. She moved into the kitchen, continuing her conversation over her shoulder.

"Will you at least listen?"

"Listen? What else have you let me do? Do you realize that this is New Year's Day and I'm missing all the college bowl games?"

"If it hadn't been for me, you'd have missed a lot more. Besides, what about the Falcons? Don't they play or practice or something today?"

"I'm injured, remember? Bum knee. The most important thing in my life right now is to find some beer and pizza. Then I'll turn on the TV and watch the Rose Parade. If you really want to stay, fine. You pop the corn, and I'll call for the food and drinks."

He started for the phone, praying that the lines were still up and that he could find somebody somewhere who would deliver.

"No pizza. If you're hungry, I've made a pot of soup."

Joe groaned. "Nobody eats soup when they watch a football game. Chili, maybe. Buffalo wings, beer, and women. That's the menu."

"Sorry, no chili, no buffalo wings, and I'm the only woman here."

"Aren't you worried about that?" he asked. "Being alone with me?"

"Yes," she admitted. "But I don't think you'll hurt me."

His expression turned cold. "Don't be so sure, Goldy. I hurt people close to me. You don't know me."

"I'm going to learn about you, Joe Armstrong, and I'm going to help you learn about you too."

"And how are you going to do that, Golden Girl?"

Annie dropped her head, concentrating on trying to open the sealed package of crackers. "Darn packaging," she muttered. "You'd think they didn't want you to eat these things."

"Goldy, look at me."

He didn't move away from the door. In fact, he had taken a step back. Why then did she feel the heat of his smile, the intensity of his vision, an insistence that wasn't going away?

Balefully she raised her gaze to meet his.

"Now, you're not really coming on to me, are you?"

"Of course not."

"Then what are we doing here?"

There was a sudden current of hot air that seemed to curl around her. Her cheeks began to burn and her blood seemed to thicken and puddle in her lower body. What was happening?

What was happening was that theirs was turning into a sensual exchange. She couldn't keep it on a professional level because she couldn't ignore her own unexpected response.

She could see it happening again—failure—this time because of her own response instead of her client's. After everything that had been done for her, she couldn't even save one ex–football star who was making himself his own next victim. No! It wasn't going to happen. She had a debt to repay, and this man was going to be her means to do it.

"Joe, help me," she blurted out, "somebody sent me to you. Somebody who cares about you more than you care about yourself. Someone who refuses to allow you to kill yourself when you still have something to give. You're not going to be lost. I won't allow you to fail because of my hang-ups."

"Whoa! Didn't anybody ever tell you that you could just say no?"

"What you and I might feel for each other under other circumstances is unimportant. I'm here for a greater purpose. Now we can do this the easy way, or we can do it the hard way. But I can tell you this, Bucko, I'm the last train to redemption and you'd better not miss me."

"Enough," he said quietly. "My mind may be dead, but my body isn't. But I'm not about to go where I'm not invited."

She walked away from the table and looked out the window. Icicles on the frames had started to melt. The water ran down the glass and formed a constant drip, melting a hole in the snow below. Everywhere there was a shine to the whiteness, a shine that, come evening, would glaze over and refreeze, making the surfaces even more treacherous than they were now. "I know this doesn't make any sense."

"Then you'd better explain."

"I wish I could, but I can't."

"So I'm supposed to welcome you into my house, without question, to do—exactly what?"

"Make you a productive human being again."

"Oh, gee. That's great. You're going to become not only my nanny, but my guru and my coach. Wow!" He took a long, hard look at her. "I'm sorry, Goldy. In spite of my protesting, I might have been open to a bit of fun and games, but all that other stuff—that's too heavy. I think you'd better get your things. You're getting out of here—now."

"What's the matter, are you afraid of me?"

"No," he said softly, pausing a long time before he continued. "I'm afraid of me. I told you, everyone close to me comes to a bad end. I appreciate a good joke as much as the next fellow," he said, "but it's time for you to fly away and find another place to do your thing."

"I can't go. I don't have a car."

"Don't worry. I'll take you. Since you took it upon yourself to sanitize my house, I need to make a little trip to the store anyway."

"Store—yes—good idea," she said, grasping for a way to stop him. "We need some basics. We'll go shopping."

Annie reached for the jacket she'd brought in when she'd rescued her suitcase from beneath a snow mound at the end of the drive.

Joe shook his head. He wasn't hallucinating. He

hadn't had a drop since midnight. He'd even gotten down one piece of toast and a cup of coffee—temporarily. But he felt as if he were in the center of a carousel that was moving around and around, totally out of control. He could slow it down but couldn't stop it.

"At the risk of voicing more useless concerns, Goldy, I just fired you from your self-appointed position as my nanny."

"You can't fire me. You didn't hire me. And I'm staying. You need me and"—she caught his arm and admitted—"I need you. Please don't send me away."

There was a kind of fear in her eyes, a need that he responded to in spite of his gruff words. It didn't make any sense. He was allowing her to steamroll him. She was tunnel-visioned, and he seemed to be the light at the end of her tunnel.

"Please?" he repeated, slipping on his jacket and stocking cap. "I'll admit last night is a bit dim, but while I'm driving you into town, let's review the evening. First, I have a name. It's Joe, Joe Armstrong. And you have a name. Surely you must have shared it with me, but I don't seem to remember. What is it?"

She brushed past him and opened the door, trying to decide how to answer him.

"Don't—" He was too late. She'd stepped off the stoop and into the snow-covered planter beside the entrance, crying out in surprise as she began to fall.

Automatically, Joe scooped her up and carried her back into the house.

"Put me down, Joe. This isn't necessary."

"Be still. You wanted to go, we're going down the steps to the garage. I do have indoor stairs, in case of sudden, unexpected snowstorms and invasions by enemy snow angels."

Her heart was pounding as she forced herself to glance up at the object of her frustration. She knew immediately that she'd made a mistake. She was having trouble breathing and it wasn't a result of being held too tightly. This was a factor she hadn't counted on—one she didn't want.

"Please let me go."

"Not until you give me a name."

Almost inaudibly she said, "Annie."

Joe nodded. "Just Annie? Not Angelique or Ann Marie?"

"Annabelle. But I go by Annie. Just plain Annie Calloway."

He kicked the kitchen door closed behind him, stepped into the narrow passageway that contained the washer and dryer, and opened what she'd thought was a storage room at the end of the hall. With his shoulder he pushed on the light switch and started down, still carrying her in his arms.

"There is nothing plain about you, Annie," he said. "Trust me, I know plain when I see it, and you don't qualify."

"Joe, you're injured, remember? I can walk." She was too conscious of the subtle masculine smell of him, of the strength in his arms, of the warmth of his breath against her hair. Her breath kicked in fast and shallow. She closed her eyes, willing herself to think of beaches and waves gently lapping at the shore.

"Walk?" he repeated. "I thought you must have wings, since there is no sign of a car, and no woman could have walked from the highway in those shoes you were wearing last night."

Mercifully they'd reached the garage and Joe's Jeep. He opened the door, hesitated a minute, then deposited her inside. After a long, searching, up-close look, he made his way to the other side and climbed in.

Separation didn't help. The beach scene refused to be calm, and her gentle waves were beginning to boil. She felt like a cup of cappuccino with a frothy head of heat anointing her brow. This was not supposed to be happening. This kind of physical reaction died in her three years earlier.

Moments later the garage door slid open, allowing the snow piled against it to collapse inside and the wind to sweep it across the concrete.

Joe concentrated on negotiating their exit. "I'm still having a hard time believing this snow," Joe said. "Do you always set off a storm?"

Annie focused on his words, forcing herself to answer slowly and logically. "No! At least I don't mean to, but things always seem to happen. Please give me a chance to make things right."

Joe put the Jeep in reverse and began backing

out of the garage. "Why is it so important for you to be here, Annie?"

"Because you need me to be here, Joe."

"What makes you so sure?"

She searched for a way to convince him. "What did you do last night before I came?"

That question stopped him cold. He honestly didn't remember. He'd had the television on. What had he watched? The only thing he could remember was the Scotch and waiting for that apple to fall. Then the doorbell had rung, and he'd opened the door to find Annie standing there with snow in her hair.

"I don't—"

"Remember," she finished for him. "And that's the last time you're going to have a night like that. That's why I'm here, Joe."

He hit the brakes and turned toward Annie. "To restore my memory?"

"No, to help you make new memories, memories you'll want to keep."

"You can never erase the past and memories can't be coerced into being," he said, "not even by you."

"Oh, yes, you *can* erase the past. I won't accept that kind of doomed talk. I won't."

"So you think that it's just a matter of living a clean life and everything will be forgiven?"

"I hope so. You just have to have a little help from someone who believes."

"Yech! She's not only a figment of my imagination, she's a figment of her own. Get real, Golden Girl. Life sucks."

"That's true," she admitted. She understood what he was feeling. She'd been there. Even now she wasn't very far away. The promise of building memories was fragile, but it was all she had, all they both had.

"Let's go find a store, Joe, with a health-food section. I'm going to buy some ginseng," she said, putting her fears behind her by meeting them head on.

He narrowed his eyes suspiciously. "Ginseng? What for?"

"Endurance," she answered. She just hoped he didn't ask what kind.

The highway was empty. Joe couldn't decide whether it was because of the weather or the holiday. He couldn't decide whether his actions were because of his hangover or his mental state.

He didn't have to drive into town. He could have found another way to get food. His regular delivery boy would have managed to make it; he liked Joe's generous tips.

Tips. In a sudden flashback, he recalled reaching for his wallet often in the last block of fuzzy time. He didn't know if he had money. Reaching for his wallet, he allowed the Jeep to swerve, and they almost ended up in a ditch.

"Careful," Annie cautioned. "I don't want to lose you now that we're on the way back."

"Back to where?" he asked as he pulled the wallet out and probed the bill compartment. There were still several bills left. Enough, he hoped, to buy whatever it was his miniature jailer had on her shopping list.

"To life. Oh, Joe, you have no idea how good it is to reach out and find something worth holding on to. Oh, look."

He followed the line of her vision and saw a flock of geese flying just over the treetops. "Geese. They're probably heading for the lake behind my house. A flock of them winter there every year."

"You know that they mate for life?" Annie asked.

The V-shaped flock disappeared behind the tall pine trees. Joe had to admit that he felt a flash of envy every time he saw them in flight. Unlike the football he threw, they could still soar on the wind. "Mate for life? Can't say I knew that. Is it important?"

She let out a quick sigh. "To me it is. Can we walk down to the lake and see them when we get back?"

Without realizing what he was committing to until after he'd spoken, he said, "Sure. But it's a steep path for someone who isn't in good shape."

She grinned at him, deliberately misunderstanding. "Don't worry. When I get done with you, you'll be able to walk miles. It's just a matter of cleaning out your system and getting you on a diet of natural foods."

Joe groaned. "I do not eat seaweed, or drink carrot juice or any other weird stuff. Meat and potatoes, that's it."

She gave him a withering look, settling her gaze on the extra pounds that had settled in at his waistline. "I can tell. But don't worry, we'll fix that. I'm a great cook."

"So far you've sold yourself as a coach, trainer, cook, housekeeper, and drill sergeant. What else?"

"What else do you need?" she asked innocently, glad that he finally seemed to be taking her assignment so well.

He liked sparring with her. She challenged him. "The body has many needs, Annie. You've overlooked a major one."

"What?"

"Sex."

She'd acknowledged that there was something between them, with her actions if not her words. Still, the look of pure terror that crossed her face was such a shock that he almost let go of the wheel in the middle of the road to reach for her. Instead, he took the first exit and came to a stop in the parking area of a strip mall that announced it was open in spite of the weather.

"Hey," he said softly. "I was only teasing. Don't panic on me, Annie."

He'd taken her hand and began rubbing it as if she'd been frostbitten and he was trying to bring life back to her icy limbs. "I'm no pervert, but I'm no knight in shining armor either. If we're playing some kind of game, you'd better tell me the rules. Otherwise I'll blow it."

"Game?" She blinked, watching his actions as if the hand being massaged belonged to someone else.

Joe didn't believe her story about being sent to retrieve him from hell, but it was obvious that she did. She wasn't after special favors for herself, no matter what she might claim. For reasons he couldn't define, he knew that he could hurt her. And he'd done enough of that. It was time to get real.

"Listen, Annie, my mama taught me to be a gentleman. Starting off the new year with you is nice, but it's just one day. When it's over, we'll let it go before both of us end up somewhere we don't want to be."

"My mother was always superstitious," she whispered. "She thought that what you did the first day of a new year was a sample of the rest. I refuse to fail."

Fail? He didn't have a clue what she was talking about. But he could tell she didn't want to be touched. He dropped her hand. "Sorry. I know you don't want me manhandling you for the rest of the year, so I'll just let you go."

"She always cooked cabbage and black-eyed peas with hog jowls. The cabbage represented money; it's green, you know. And the black-eyed peas and pork brought you luck."

"And did it?" he asked curiously. He couldn't believe that every time he had a chance to get out, he continued to extend their conversation. She was a stranger, yet he felt a kind of kinship that was downright dumb. "Bring you wealth and good luck?"

She might have said no. But there was a time when she'd been very wealthy and her luck had carried her to places she'd dreamed of but never expected to go. "Yes, it did."

"You don't sound very pleased about it."

"Oh, I am. At least I'm pleased with it now. And I suppose I was then, at least until things went bad."

"I don't guess you'd like to tell me what went bad?"

She shook her head, gradually regrouping and pulling her resolve together. "No, not yet. Maybe later. Let's get our food."

"Yeah, we need some wealth and good luck. Besides, we're missing the Sugar Bowl." Big deal, he decided, it seemed to be important to her that she spend the day with him. It would be a way to fill the empty time. He'd go along.

"No," she quipped in that wide-eyed way she had of misunderstanding, "I'm certain there was a sugar bowl in your cupboard."

"Game, not bowl." Joe laughed and let his foot off the brake, driving across the shopping center to stop in front of the grocery chain store. "I hope you made a list, because I sure as hell don't know what you need."

"I don't need a list," she said in a low voice as she climbed out of the Jeep. "I know what I need. I just wish I could get it in a store."

FOUR

Inside the store, Joe followed Annie around as she put things in the grocery cart. He watched, but his mind was still on the expression on her face when he'd mentioned sex.

Given her age—about twenty-eight or so, he guessed—and her looks, he couldn't believe that she was some kind of ice cube. He'd thought at first that she was someone's practical joke, but she was too determined for that.

Then he'd considered that she was simply working on her own, trying to burrow her way into his life. But so far she'd avoided every opportunity for intimacy. None of these scenarios really fit. He'd been out of the locker-room scene too long for his old buddies to be playing jokes. Even Rob wouldn't try something like this.

It was as if Joe had fallen into some kind of dream and couldn't wake up. Even now, there was something appealing about following Annie around the store, almost as if they'd done this before. Almost as if they were a couple of ordinary people leading ordinary lives. And he didn't like the ease with which she fitted into his.

Still, she'd admitted that someone had sent her. If that person wasn't someone he knew, then she had to be working for a really strange kind of operation, maybe even a cult. He'd read about weird groups that focused on wealthy people who were vulnerable for some reason or other.

She paused at the produce counter, then reached for a large purple vegetable that looked more like something out of *Invasion of the Body Snatchers* than edible produce.

"I hope you're not planning to buy that," he said.

"Of course. Eggplant is a great source of vitamin A."

"Eggplants? What kind of sick chicken is responsible for that? And who on earth would want to grow it?"

Annie struggled to hold back a laugh. He liked the sound of her laughter; it was as normal as the rest of the scene in which she'd cast them. She must have seen a softening in his face, because she shook her head and reluctantly put the vegetable back.

"All right, we'll start out simpler. We'll get broccoli, carrots, zucchini, and some greens."

Joe groaned. "No zucchini, please. I filled my zucchini quota years ago. It was served at every sports banquet I ever attended. Even if I had liked it to start with, I wouldn't now."

"You haven't eaten my zucchini. I'm a great cook, Joe. That's one thing I don't screw up."

He refrained from repeating her words, changing his question so that he wouldn't bring back her stricken look. "I guess it would be easy to make mistakes in your line of work. I mean, if you dropped in on the wrong person, you could get yourself killed."

The camaraderie that had been building between them died and that frozen look of horror swept over her face again, removing every tinge of color. He was surprised the carrots she was holding didn't change from orange to white.

"All my clients are thoroughly checked out in advance," she said through clenched teeth. "Any tendency toward violence is carefully considered and appropriate measures are taken."

"Straight out of the course manual for Crime Fighters 101. Are you a cop?"

She gave a weak laugh. "No. I'm scared to death of guns."

"A doctor, then, one of those who puts people back together mentally."

The color was returning to her face. "Not exactly. I flunked biology twice."

What was left? Joe was back to his original thought—a member of a cult. Here he was, standing in the produce department of a supermarket on

New Year's Day with a beautiful woman who had already admitted she was after his soul.

"I hate to ask, but you don't belong to a gang, do you?"

She frowned. "A gang? Goodness, no."

Joe's sigh of relief was almost comical.

Annie slapped a bunch of celery in the basket and moved briskly toward the fruit. She leaned over and examined a basket of red apples. "These will help to rid your system of all impurities."

Joe watched the way her running suit cupped her bottom. He felt at least one of his impurities begin to stir, and he didn't think food would take care of the problem.

"Apples, I like," he said, ripping a plastic bag from the roll and holding it open for her to fill. Bags of grapefruit, pears, and grapes followed. Then she stopped at the specialties counter and picked up a clear plastic container of what looked like rotten cheese. When she added that to the cart, he took hold of the handle and refused to allow it to move.

"What is that?"

"That's tofu," she said with a wide smile. "And these"—she lifted another container and placed it inside—"are bean sprouts."

"And this"—Joe picked up and identified his selection—"is caramel to be melted so that our apples and our popcorn can be dipped. And nuts, we need some nuts. They're healthy, aren't they?"

She nodded yes to his question. "Yes, except

let's buy walnuts instead of peanuts. I'll use them in other dishes. But put back the caramels. Too much sugar."

Joe had had enough. "I don't think so, Annie. We've already passed on the steak and roast beef in favor of chicken and seafood, and the fish wasn't even catfish. I guess I can assume that we aren't going down the chips-and-beer aisle, are we?"

"You can assume that."

"I suppose you're going to stock up on mineral water and cereal that looks like grass and twigs?"

"You may."

"Well, I hate to tell you, but you may as well forget about that ginseng. I'll never have the strength to make use of it."

At the dairy counter, Annie added skim milk and juice, then stopped and faced her client. He'd been surprisingly good-natured about their shopping expedition so far. Maybe she ought to allow him one treat of his own choosing. After all, he was paying.

"Okay, Joe. You may pick something sweet. Let's get some yogurt and some fruit bars."

"You get yogurt. I'm getting ice cream and doughnuts." With that he opened the glass ice-cream locker and swept out several cartons without even looking. Next he pushed the cart past the deli and settled on the doughnuts and pastries. Anything that had icing went in the basket. Finally, he was satisfied that he'd proved his point and started toward the checkout counter.

Annie followed meekly, watching in amusement as the few shoppers cleared a path for the big athlete. She allowed herself to let go for a minute and watch him. If she'd thought this job would be easy, she was wrong. Joe Armstrong might believe himself to be a washed-up athlete, but he was still a very attractive man. She hadn't expected him to have a sense of humor; something she'd been told she didn't have. And she hadn't expected to respond to him as a woman. Lordy, she didn't need that. She certainly couldn't allow any long-closed-off feelings she had to come back to life—even if her doctor had told her that one day she'd begin to feel again.

Annie Calloway didn't want to feel. The absence of emotion made life easier. Her doctor might think her full recovery would eventually demand a normal sexual relationship, but if Mac found out she had such a thing with Joe, he'd haul her back to the mountaintop in a flash.

The whispers of the shoppers continued. They didn't have to know who Joe was to know he was somebody special. Once Annie had enjoyed that kind of notoriety—enjoyed, then endured it. After her trouble she'd lightened her hair and gained enough weight to protect her identity. Being anonymous was better.

"You know, you didn't buy any black-eyed peas or hog jowls," Joe commented as the clerk scanned their selections. "No good luck and wealth for us this year?"

"Is that what you want, Joe?"

He frowned. "Money? No, I've had that. Good luck, maybe, but at this point that may be pushing the envelope. Perhaps I'm doomed to zucchini and mineral water forever. Wouldn't that be hell?"

Joe stacked the doughnuts and caramels neatly beside all the healthy food Annie had bought. The checkout clerk glanced at them and smiled at Joe as if she knew who had picked what.

"I could deal with that," he mused. "Scotch, a New Year's Eve party for one, and an angel moving in. And all the time I thought hell would be fire and brimstone."

Day one of hell. She almost nodded. He'd figure out sooner or later that this was day one on his journey out of hell. January 1. The first day of her assignment. Only five more days to go.

Hell—she used Joe's own expletive. At least he was confused and intrigued. By the end of the week he'd be plenty tired of fun and games. She'd better have come up with some way to keep him interested long enough for her to complete her job.

She didn't know anything about football, so that was out. It was apparent from his condo that she and Joe didn't share any hobbies. In fact, she didn't think he had any. There was no stereo and no collection of CDs, and the only videotapes she'd found were replays of the Falcon games. There were no books, and she'd bet the television dish outside the window was set to pick up every sports event in the country. They must share some kind of common ground. But what?

Joe paid for the groceries and flung the bags in the Jeep, then drove rapidly away from the shopping center and back toward the condo with little regard for the snow.

"You drive as if you've spent time in snow country," she ventured. "Have you?"

"Some, and I've spent time in Hawaii and Texas too. When you play sports, you travel."

"Oh, is that why you aren't settled in your house yet?"

He moved across a dirty mound of snow to find the melting rut in the center, then relaxed as the vehicle moved forward. "I'm settled in. Why did you think otherwise?"

"Well, it's a bit bare. Don't you—I mean, what did you do when you weren't playing football?"

"Nothing."

"No hobbies?"

"No hobbies. What about you? What do you do when you aren't tormenting football players?"

"I—I torment other people."

"What about before?"

She weighed her options. A certain amount of truth ought to be acceptable. "Before, I was a model."

His eyes widened. *"Playboy?"*

"The Sears Roebuck catalog. And a few other assignments."

He looked at her again. "I can't help but think

I've seen you before. Are you sure we've never met?"

She'd better change the subject. Too much truth could be a problem. "I'm sure. Now, let's talk about debts, Joe."

"Sure, nothing like a sparkling conversation about debts for a man with a headache and a hazy memory."

"I'm sorry. Would you like some aspirin?"

"No, I'd like a drink."

"Talk to me about money, Joe. How are you fixed financially?"

It was a bold question. She wanted to know if he was wealthy; he'd tell her.

"I'm fine. I may have messed up my life, but I had the good fortune to have a dad who gave me sound advice: Save your money before you spend it."

"Sounds like a wise man, all right. I'm sorry about what happened to him. Both your folks dying at one time must have been dreadful."

Joe jerked around, his surprise almost physical. "What do you know about my folks?"

"I know you lost them both in an accident. That's hard. But at least your dad helped you prepare for the future. Being financially set has a lot to do with a person's recovery."

"What is this, a marketing survey or a credit report? I'm not in any kind of financial trouble. If you're looking for a loan, I might consider it. What about your debts?"

"My debt is greater than you'll ever understand, Joe. Please, talking this out is important. I probably know most of your history, but I have to hear it from you."

"It's that important to you, huh?"

"It is."

"Then let's negotiate. I'll consider cooperating with you, if you'll cooperate with me."

She didn't like the sound of that, but short of telling him everything, which she'd been severely cautioned not to do, she couldn't see any other way to break down his barriers.

"All right, we'll negotiate. State your terms."

"I'll have to think about them," he said slowly. "After all, you had advance warning. This is new to me. About my debts, I don't have any, at least none to speak of. My house is paid for. My Jeep's paid for. Wherever I go, people seem to want to pay for my travel and my meals. It makes them happy, so I let them. Anything wrong with that?"

She could have told him that once she'd traveled that same risky road, but he wouldn't understand the risks because he hadn't reached the end of it yet.

Annie glanced out the window at the tall pines tucked between pockets of farmland, trees drooping with snow that had begun to fall in great plops to the ground. They turned off the highway and headed down a side road, where, in past times, the tree limbs would have folded themselves over the route, making a tent under which the car traveled.

Electric lines marred one side of the road now, cutting back the leaves. The scene resembled the face of a man who'd shaved on one side only.

Though he'd been intrigued in the beginning, Joe was beginning to worry about her proprietary attitude. He was ready to get back to the condo, turn on the game, and rear back in his easy chair. He ought to stop the Jeep and let Little Miss Sunbeam fly away to wherever she'd come from and take her tofu and bean sprouts with her.

But he didn't.

"I need some answers, Goldy," he said finally.

She let out a silent sigh of relief at his statement. Maybe he was going to cooperate. "If I can," she agreed.

"Where did you come from?"

"Originally from Texas, then New York. Most recently, Memphis, Tennessee. Is this part of the negotiations?"

That wasn't what he'd meant, but it was a start. He nodded. "What did you do, then?"

"The same thing I'm doing here, helping someone who needed me. It's very beautiful up here, Joe. I'm surprised. I expected you to live in one of those swinging-singles complexes or a mansion around some fancy golf course."

"You don't have a very high opinion of me, do you?"

She swung around to face him, drawing one leg beneath her. "I don't judge my clients, Joe. What's more important is what *you* think of you."

He groaned. "Is that a heavenly chorus I hear behind you? I expect to see you unfurl your wings and ascend into the heavens at any moment."

Annie gave a little gasp. "Joe, don't make me something I'm not. I don't have wings."

"Then how'd you get to my house last night? You were obviously looking for me. I wasn't a random choice. Except for the fast-food delivery boys nearby, very few people know where I live. But you found me, in the dark, in a snowstorm. And you have no car."

"I had help—from an associate."

"Then your associate must be Superman or the devil," he said, and turned off the expressway onto the road that carried them back up the mountain. "By the way, if all those questions about money mean you're planning to rob me, forget it. This is a holiday weekend and the bank is closed. I don't have an ATM card. Every penny I have is here in my wallet."

So that was why he'd asked about a gang. "I don't need your money, Joe. I have plenty of my own. I earned it the hard way. Athletes aren't the only ones who learn they won't always be on top and prepare for when they aren't."

"*Dum dum da-dum.*" He began to drone on in the rhythm of a funeral dirge. "From the whirl of wings we fade to the sound of adding machines and computers. What other words of wisdom are you planning to share?"

"You said we'd negotiate, Joe. I'm willing. I

know you don't understand, but I have to do this for you. I need to succeed. Please, let me try."

Her words were almost desperate. All the sunshine was gone, along with the perky voice and the take-charge manner. She was staring at him intently, clasping her hands so tightly that they were white across the knuckles. Whatever her game was, she was good at it, for even though he knew he was being conned, he couldn't figure out how. He was becoming even more intrigued, and that was something he hadn't felt in a very long time.

So, what should he do?

She was beautiful. She was determined to bulldoze him, and she could cook, or so she said. And she was apparently about to become his new housemate, whether he was agreeable or not.

He took another look at her golden hair and her peaches-and-cream complexion and decided that he was only fooling himself about his reluctance.

So he'd always been a sucker for a mystery. What the hell. What else did he have to do for the rest of his life? He might as well see how far she'd go with the wild scheme, whatever it was.

They reached the house. He drove into the garage, let the door down behind him, and thought about what he was going to say.

"I can't figure you out, Goldy, but maybe that doesn't matter. It seems to be big-time important to you that you become my new personal keeper. I don't know where you're going with it, but at the moment there isn't much happening in my life that

I can't get back to later. So, come on in and whip up some rotten cheese and bean sprouts."

The look of relief that she turned on him was almost worth the skepticism he'd felt.

"Thank you, Joe. You won't regret this. I promise."

He would regret it. As soon as he'd agreed, he knew he would. Now his head was really pounding.

"The only thing I regret is that we just missed the kickoff and I let you talk me out of getting beer. That rotten cheese better be good."

It was time for Annie to report in. She'd thought she might manage to call from the store, but Joe had followed her around like a lost puppy. Now she had no choice. Unless she called Mac, he'd send someone to check on her.

"I'll put the groceries away and reheat the soup. You go on in and turn on your game," she said, giving Joe a shove through the door.

"I have to eat soup?"

"You do. But first I'll brew you a cup of herbal tea and help you get rid of your headache."

Joe put the bags of groceries on the counter and headed for his easy chair. His head was really pounding, and he couldn't be certain whether it was the lack of food or overindulgence in drink. Either way, past experience told him that only time would help.

He didn't count on Annie. She appeared with a

cup of steaming tea, which she made him drink all at once. Then she came to stand behind him.

"Turn the sound down a bit so it won't override my touch," she said, then reached for the remote and adjusted it herself when he made no move to follow directions.

"Hey, wait just a minute. I want to hear this."

"And you will, in a lot less discomfort. Lean back, Joe."

Anything to get her to the kitchen and away from the start of the second quarter. Auburn was playing Penn State. Auburn, just off probation, had gone undefeated, but nobody thought they were any good. Like the Falcons, they were a Cinderella team, and at the moment they were behind.

"Lean back, Joe," she repeated, and placed both hands on his forehead, her fingertips meeting in the middle. She let them rest there for a long minute, generating a kind of energy that seemed to draw from the rest of his body. Then she began to massage his head, around his ears, and down the sides of his neck.

"Feel the light, Joe. Feel it leave my fingers and sink into your head, like little spears of heat seeking out the pain, absorbing it, and leaving only gentle peace behind it. Feel the pain go, Joe. There is only warmth and serenity. Rest, Joe. Give me your pain."

Moments later he was sleeping, yet not sleeping at all. He was watching the game, but he felt as if he were suspended in a gentle wind that rocked him like a child being held by its mother.

He'd never felt anything quite like it. He'd never known anyone quite like Annie. Then the crowd noise rose and he was drawn into the game. It was the end of the quarter when he realized that Annie was gone.

"Mac? I'm here."

"It's about time. What about our boy?"

"He's about half-asleep, watching one of those ball games."

"Has he accepted you?" the familiar voice asked.

"Not entirely. He thinks I'm either after his body or his money. The women in his life haven't been casual about their interests."

"I can't imagine that he doesn't like you, Annie."

"That's just it, I think he's afraid he might."

"Do I detect a hint of personal interest on your part?"

"Mac, this is a personal business. But you of all people should understand that any relationship is out of the question. That part of my life is over."

"I understand, Annie. I'll leave the method of communication up to you. But remember, we only delayed the inevitable for six days. If you don't pull him back by then, we've lost him."

Annie sighed and glanced through the crack in

the door to make sure that her target was still where she'd left him. "I know, Mac. I'll work it out, I promise. I just don't know how. The man is— was—a football player and, as far as I can tell, nothing else."

"Then play with him. You'll think of something."

"I know," she whispered, and hung up the phone. "I just wish I knew what."

She put away the food, reheated the soup, and found bowls in which to serve it. Considering Joe's physical state, she added dry crackers and a glass of artificially sweetened iced tea. Behind the kitchen door she found a set of TV trays and set up two of them.

She placed the soup bowls, glasses, and crackers on the trays. Then, with a smile, she reached back and added two apples.

The chicken soup would give Joe nourishment, and the spices would cover the natural herbs she'd added to the mix. Glancing out the window, she noted how dark it was getting. The sun was gone and with it the warmth. The rattle of a branch against the window announced that the wind was rising, and the length of the icicles indicated that the runoff had begun to refreeze.

At least that took some of the pressure away, she thought as she picked up Joe's tray and pushed open the kitchen door. If the roads were freezing over, he couldn't expect her to leave.

If the herbs she'd added to the soup worked, he wouldn't ask her to.

"Who's winning?" she asked as she placed the tray in front of Joe.

He started. He didn't know. For a moment he tried to replay the last quarter in his mind, but it was all a blur. "What did you do to me?" he asked.

"Didn't your headache go away?"

"Yeah, that and the ball game too. I sat here and watched it, and I don't even know who's winning."

"You just took a quick nap, Joe. You should be fine for the rest of the evening."

"How'd you do that, Annie?"

"It's just a relaxation technique someone taught me. I'll teach you when you're ready. Eat."

He was almost afraid to taste the soup. After what had happened with the tea, he was liable to sleep for a hundred years or something equally bizarre. He'd just refuse. But she sat in the chair on the other side of the lamp table and watched him, waiting for him to comply.

Dutifully, with the idea of resisting but without the ability to do so, he lifted the spoon and tasted the soup. "Hey, this is good."

"I told you I'm a good cook." She smiled and began to eat her own. "I won't start you on the new regimen until tomorrow. I'll make us an omelette later, if you're still hungry."

He was afraid to ask what kind of ingredients she planned to use. Instead he assured her, "I'll be hungry about Orange Bowl time. Say, what was in that tea you gave me?"

"Just plain old herbal tea from your canister."

He would have argued, but he couldn't be sure whether it was Annie or the tea that was having such a strange effect on him. His skin tingled and the warmth of her caress was as real as if she were still touching him.

Joe ate the soup and the crackers and took a bite of the apple before the answer came to him. Even his father understood that there were mystical events that influenced lives beyond what man understood. Nothing else made any sense.

All that mumbo jumbo, touching him, brewing liquids.

The woman was a witch.

FIVE

Joe finished off the soup and watched the rest of the game. He'd expected Annie's presence to intrude. But it hadn't. He'd expected her to find a reason to cross-examine him or test him in some way.

The woman didn't fidget or find some irritating activity to engage in to take his attention from the television. Though she'd said they'd make some kind of plan, she seemed content to sit and watch with him, interrupting only to ask about a play. Her willingness simply to enjoy the game finally became more of a distraction than conversation.

"You don't know much about football, do you?" he asked.

"No. I wasn't into sports much as a child."

"No brother who played, or a boyfriend?"

"No. I was an only child. My stepmother didn't believe in sports. I always worked."

There was something odd about her answer. He thought about it for a moment and decided that it was the tone of her voice rather than the words she'd spoken.

"You lived with your father?"

"Until he disappeared and left me with my stepmother. My mother skipped out when I was four years old. My dad waited another six years. Never heard from either one of them again."

He sat up in his chair. "Damn! That's hard to believe."

"Believe it, it happens. But it was okay. I had it rough, but I survived."

She might think she was tough, but Joe had a feeling that her toughness went about as deep as his bravado. They were both fakes.

"I'm sorry, Annie. My dad was pretty strict. It wasn't easy being the preacher's kid, and there were times I wished I was an orphan. But he was there. My mama was too. They were my motivation. What was yours?"

"To be somebody. That was all I ever wanted. To have the world see Annabelle Calloway and say, Wow!"

"Wow!" Joe responded, and waited for her to say something. She didn't. So he continued to look at her. If he had to have a nanny, he was glad that it was Annie who'd come to take him in hand. Obviously she'd achieved her goal. Which again brought up the nagging question of why she was there. "You know"—he leaned back in his recliner and turned the sound back up a notch—"coming from one who's been there, being on top ain't what it's cracked up to be."

He almost didn't hear her "I know."

Somewhere about halftime of the final bowl game, he drank the second cup of herbal tea she brought and mellowed out entirely. He even started to doze. When she finally woke him, he found out he'd missed the last quarter of the game, and, amazingly enough, he didn't care. She stood and waited as he started up the stairs.

"Good night, Joe."

He stopped abruptly at the top and turned back. "I'm sorry. I didn't even think, I mean, about sleeping arrangements. I'll take the couch."

She shook her head. "That isn't necessary. I think you're a little long for the couch. I slept fine down here last night. But I could use a pillow."

Still caught in that bemused aura halfway between being fully awake and asleep, Joe tested his lips with a quirky grin. "My mama always taught me to share."

"Good. Give me one from your bed. I found an extra blanket." She started up the steps behind him. As she reached the top he said, "That wasn't quite what I had in mind. I wouldn't want you to think I'm a poor host. You can have half my bed."

"Thank you, Joe, but no thanks. It isn't allowed."

He shrugged his shoulders. "That's what I thought you'd say." He went into his bedroom and tugged one of the pillows from beneath the bed-spread and held it out. "Too bad."

When she reached for the pillow, he didn't let go. Instead he stepped closer, studying her in the light from the hall. "Don't suppose you'd do a little bartering, would you? I mean, I've been coopera-tive, haven't I?"

"I—I suppose you have."

"And I haven't tried to throw you out once to-night, have I? I'll even promise to listen to your schedule tomorrow."

"Thank you." Her heart rate had increased alarmingly, not to the point where she'd turn and run away, but she felt a definite excitement. Expect-ing it to change any minute, she simply stood, as if their shared hold on the pillow was some kind of promise. They'd spent an entire day together and it was obvious that while he wasn't yet ready to accept her, at least he was willing to listen.

And, to her surprise, she hadn't bolted from his touch.

Still fighting the expected sense of panic to overwhelm her, she waited. It didn't happen. As he lowered his face toward hers she didn't move. Somehow, the pillow between them cushioned any threat she might have imagined.

Their lips touched, briefly, like butterfly wings brushing, then moving away. Her eyes fluttered closed. Amazingly, her pulse slowed. Her lips curled into a smile.

"Good night, Annie," he whispered.

"Good night, Joe."

He placed both hands on her shoulders and turned her around, giving her a swat on the bottom. "Sweet dreams. Tomorrow is another day."

She knew that, all right. He didn't have to remind her. Tomorrow was another day, day two of her six. And she had made no real progress on her assignment. Nothing had changed for Joe. He was still the same ex-jock he'd been on New Year's Eve. Annie Calloway, on the other hand, wasn't sure that she was quite the same. She seemed to have taken a reluctant step forward.

But Annie wasn't supposed to be the focus of this retrieval.

Still, sitting there in his house, just the two of them, with the world closed off, had been nice— nonthreatening, even normal. She stopped by the bathroom, brushed her teeth, and instead of wearing her gown, she pulled on the T-shirt she'd worn the night before. As she started back downstairs she heard Joe's voice.

"I think I'd like it if the rest of the year could be anything like the first day. And we didn't even have to eat hog jowls and black-eyed peas. Too bad it won't last."

"Oh, Mac, how do I reach him?" she asked later as she made her second call of the day to report. "Without allowing it to—to become personal?"

"I can't tell you, Annie. Sometimes you have to take chances if the stakes are high enough."

"But how do I give him a tomorrow when he thinks it's been taken away?"

"Maybe you could give him part of yours, Annie," was Mac's cryptic answer.

The next morning Joe woke up ravenous. His head was clear, his energy level was up, and for the first time in months he was eager to start the day. He didn't remember a lot about the bowl games the day before; he guessed he'd been tired and had dozed through most of them.

But he remembered Annie and their good night kiss.

And he remembered his stupid conclusion that Annie Calloway was a modern-day witch. He lay there thinking for a moment. Being a witch didn't explain her reaction to his mention of sex—everybody knew that witches engaged in depraved orgies—and it didn't explain what she wanted, or why their day together had been so nice.

He sprang out of bed, pulled on a pair of jeans, dug a shirt out of the closet, and went looking for her in spite of the solemn vow he'd made that he wouldn't get close to anybody—ever again. *Remember, Joe, you're bad luck for the people you care about.* He didn't want anything bad to happen to Annie. Though there was an appealing thing or two he'd like to see happen, and remembering that kiss, if he played his cards just right . . .

He caught hold of the banister and slowed his pace. "Not a good idea, Armstrong. No more lies. You can't buy your way out of hell. Your chances for any sort of hereafter are already suspect, you can't afford to make another mistake."

To be sure of this, he had to do what he'd started out to do—get rid of her quick. That was why he was hurrying, he told himself. Annie had appointed herself his keeper without knowing what that entailed. He'd been too close to self-destruction the night she'd come. If he did have an accident and went off the mountain as he'd considered, he could take her with him. And the world would be darker without Annie.

To be fair, she ought to be told that she had him pegged all wrong. He was a survivor, too, albeit a reluctant one. Even worse, he was a liar. She could be the one in danger, the one who'd be hurt.

There was coffee on the stove but the house was empty. That set him back. He couldn't reconcile the hollow feeling in his gut when he realized she wasn't there.

He peered through the window to see that the snow was melting. Pausing for a second, he listened carefully, then laughed at himself as he admitted that he was listening for the sound of wings or at least a bell ringing.

Even in the worst of his recent blackouts he knew that there was no such thing as angels. Nor was there some kind of sorcerer somewhere who could zap people where he wanted them to be with a flick of a pointed finger. And witches belonged to Halloween, not the first of a new year.

But where the hell was she?

Could something have happened to her already?

Quickly he pulled on socks, shoes, and a sweatshirt with a hood. When he opened the back door, he let out an audible sigh of relief. A trail of footprints in the snow led away from the house toward the woods behind. Like a kid knowing he was heading for trouble and going anyway, he jammed his hands in his pockets and loped after her.

She was standing on the bank looking out over the lake, where the gaggle of geese they'd seen in flight were breaking the thin layer of ice and diving beneath.

"They're beautiful, aren't they, Joe?"

"I suppose. They're also foolish."

She turned to face him. "Why?"

"This area is a favorite for hunters and fishermen. Some of the geese have already been killed."

She felt a chill sweep over her. "Why do they stay?"

"I'm told it's because this is where they winter every year. Maybe it's some kind of instinct."

"Maybe it's because this is home, Joe."

"More likely it's because the guy who lived in the house across the lake used to feed them."

"And now he doesn't?"

"No. He doesn't live there anymore." *He's gone, like everything else around me*, he could have said. Except for these geese, who didn't seem to know they were taking a chance on being caught up in his jinx.

"Then we'll—*you'll* have to feed them, Joe."

He liked the sound of that *we* more than he wanted to. In fact, it forced him to remember what he'd made up his mind to do—make Annie go.

"Not us, not me. Let's go back inside, Annie. I thank you for giving me a lovely first day of the new year, but I think it's time we did some serious talking about me and you and this future you're trying to help me find."

Annie turned and followed him back to the house. He was right. Putting off the confrontation wasn't going to make it go away. She had spent a good deal of the night trying to figure out a way to make her assignment work. There appeared to be only one way, and it involved the one thing she wasn't certain she could do.

She had to make Joe want her to stay—no matter what—and he'd squashed every scenario she'd come up with, except one. The one obvious common element was the pure physical attraction that flared between them. The only thing he'd offered to barter for was sex.

But for her, sex was not allowed. It was the one thing a retriever was unequivocally forbidden to use. No, that wasn't precisely right. Sex wasn't spelled out in the contract. The actual wording was, *You will neither fall in love with your client nor use sex for personal gain.*

In Annie's mind, sex was synonymous with love, and she already knew that she couldn't indulge in sex, even if she got past her fear. Reconstructing a physical relationship wasn't the same as creating a new face. The absence of sex eliminated the possibility of love. But sex seemed to be the only sure way to reach the man.

"Joe," she said, "I don't know how, but I have to find a way to make you accept the offer I want to make."

He stopped and turned back, a traitorous smile curling his lips. She was so beautiful, so serious. He couldn't seem to make his face behave. "I've got it. You're a team owner and you want me to manage the Angels?"

"Even I know that the Angels are a baseball team. You played football."

"Okay, so your team sprouts a different kind of wings. They're geese."

"My team," she said, "isn't a team at all, at least not the kind you mean. I'm on my own. There's only me—and you."

To Joe, the emphasis on the *me and you* was obvious and his immediate reaction was quick and undeniable. What in hell kind of woman was this that she only had to suggest a connection and his body surged into a heated response. "Is this part of that hot light you keep talking about, some sort of hypnotic suggestion?"

"I wish it was that easy."

She brushed past him, reaching the house first and opening the door. "First breakfast, then talk."

While Joe stamped the snow from his feet and followed her inside, she poured hot coffee in her cup, adding sugar and cream and stirring it as she tried to settle on a way to present her plan.

She walked toward the window to put some distance between them as he came in, stopping just inside the door. The snow was gone except in shady spots beneath the trees. From Joe's dining area she could see the road they'd traveled the day before, but there was little traffic. In the summer the houses on the lake were probably used. Now, in the winter, they were empty.

Another sign of Joe's pulling away from life—his isolation, though she could appreciate the quiet beauty of the stillness. A redheaded woodpecker lit on the bark of a dead tree, filling the silence with a determined *rat-a-tat-tat*. She made a note to buy birdseed, then admonished her thoughts. She wouldn't be there long enough for the birds to get used to coming for food. "And he probably wouldn't feed them when I'm gone."

"Feed who?"

He'd come up behind her silently in his stocking feet. She was surprised that she hadn't felt him close the distance between them. For now that she was aware of his presence, she knew that awareness came from more than his voice. It was that little shimmering sensation that pricked at the back of her knees. She'd come to recognize it as the "Joe response."

"The birds," she said. "Look out there, a woodpecker. I was thinking of the geese, of trying to convince you to buy seed, but I guess that's unfair."

He moved closer and looked past her. "Is this part of your plan?"

She could feel the tickle of his hair on her cheek, the warmth of his breath by her ear. She couldn't seem to stop the odd ripple of her skin. Even knowing her time was limited, she realized the assignment had become more than simply saving Joe. She wasn't ready to go further into intimacy, for she was still fighting her own demons. Yet she didn't seem to be able to avoid what was happening.

"No, I like birds," she whispered. "But I can't expect you to take care of them, and I won't be here long enough to get them used to coming. I have to accomplish my goal, and I don't have much time. Please help me, Joe."

He didn't know why her words cut into his gut with such force. Getting her out was exactly what he'd had in mind. But now that she was announcing her departure, it hit him like an arctic blast. "I don't understand. You said something before about having only a few days to redeem me. Are you giving up?"

"No, but I only have six days."

"Even the big guy took seven days to make the earth. Don't you think six days is expecting a lot?"

"Six days," she corrected. "On the seventh He rested. Let's have breakfast."

But she didn't move. To do so would have meant pushing him away or touching him, and she was afraid to do either. Her pulse was pounding so hard, she was certain that he could feel it. There was something dangerously alluring about being so close and not touching. Something she dared not give into.

Joe wasn't doing any better. He was past trying to put a name to his need to be close to her. When had he last made a rational observation about anything for himself? How could he possibly do so when the elusive scent of her was slowing every part of his mental process?

"No breakfast, Annie. No feeding the birds. I may be a dumb ex-jock, but wherever you came from, I know you're out of my league. Why are you really here?"

"I don't suppose you'd accept me as a house-keeper?"

"No."

"A secretary? A—manager?"

"Already got one."

"Maybe just a friend."

His skeptical look was answer enough. Desperately, Annie pushed past him, put down her cup, removed her jacket, and leaned back against the counter. She'd run out of options and time. If sex was her only means to reach the man, she'd have to chance it.

With her chin pressed against her neck, eyelids lowered, lips parted, breath coming in short, shallow pants, she took on the expression that had once made her famous. Now, positioning her legs so that she was standing with equal weight on both feet, she arched her hips slightly forward.

As an actress she'd spent two years playing the role of the hottest vamp on daytime TV. The media had attributed her success to a special visual sensuality. It wasn't what she looked like, but a certain way she had of using body language to appeal to a man. Satisfied that she had his total attention, she raised her eyelids and gave him "the look," the Annise trademark, guaranteed to arouse.

"Aren't you hungry, Joe?"

Joe's eyes widened. What the hell? This was a new game. This was an entirely different woman.

Annie planted her gaze on his feet and swept it upward. She didn't have to tell him to feel the light this time—it was searing his skin. His awareness of her became a physical caress, pausing now at his zipper, then moving up his chest to his face. He was on fire, caught up in an erotic fantasy such as he'd never experienced.

"What are you offering?" he asked in a tight voice.

She held her pose for a long minute, then suddenly she seemed to wilt. The vamp disappeared. And fear swept across the face of his Golden Girl.

"Oh, Joe," she said in a throaty whisper. "What

am I doing? I can't. I'm sorry. This is what I used to do, but not anymore. I'm not offering anything."

"What you used to do?" he repeated, still not sure about what he was seeing.

"Breakfast first. Then I'll explain."

"You sound like my mother," he finally said. "After I clean my plate I can have my surprise?"

"Look at me, Joe. Do I really look like your mother?"

"Look at me, Annie. Do I really look hungry for food?"

In fact, her heart was racing so fast that she was no longer acting. Her little show had had an unexpected result. She didn't know what Joe felt, but she was weak in the knees. She had to slow things down.

"Eat first, Joe. Then talk."

She prepared his food and served him, careful to avoid his touch. She couldn't tell whether the heat between them bounced off her to him or if it was the other way around.

He ate the oatmeal as he thought about her vivid invitation, then ate the raisins and the bananas as he visualized her body. He washed down the vitamins with orange juice as he mentally undressed her. Then he pushed back from the table. He didn't know what she thought she was doing, but he intended to find out.

"So, I'm buying the invitation you took back. Talk to me, Goldy."

She scooped in a desperate breath and let it go.

"I'm not supposed to tell you this, Joe, but I don't know any other way. I *was* a model once, but that wasn't all. Until three years ago I was Annise, the wild child of the soap opera *Beyond Love*. I doubt you ever watched it, but a lot of men did, a lot of crazy men who thought I was their own personal fantasy."

In spite of her sexy pitch moments earlier, as Annie talked she didn't look sexy. Before Joe's eyes she turned into a woman filled with pain, a woman determined to bare her soul for a reason he didn't yet understand. There was almost a desperation in her voice. Whatever, whoever she was, she seemed to have some crazy idea that she *had* to reach him.

Even as his long-lost instinct to be kind kicked in and made him listen, he knew he had to make her understand that he was bad news for her. She didn't deserve what was sure to happen to her if she stayed. But she was getting to him.

"I never watched the soaps, but lots of our guys did. And lots of them dated actresses too. Did you go out with one of my friends?"

"No, I was engaged to the boy from back home," she said. "We were going to be married, until—" Her voice caught in her throat.

"Until what, dammit?"

"I was being stalked by a fan, a man who became obsessed with me. I was on top of the world, and I didn't take it seriously. And then one night he broke into my apartment and he—"

Her beautiful face, the stitches. Joe remembered the story. It had been all over the news-papers; the lovely young actress who was raped, slashed, horribly mutilated by a stalker. "But I thought that she—I mean that you—"

"Died? No. I came very near death, and there were more times than I can tell you when I wished I had died. Let's just say that someone who cared about me arranged for me to disappear from the public eye. I'm not Annise anymore. I don't even look like her."

"Annie, it's hard to believe the tabloids let you get away with that."

"My guardian angel is very powerful. Because of the attack, my life was changed forever. It was a year before I even knew who I once was and what had happened to me. By then that life was gone. I'd lost my career, the man I thought I loved, and my future. I had nothing to live for."

"I know that feeling . . . well."

"Yes. I know you do. But after a time, with help, I begin to heal. At least my body did."

He lifted his puzzled expression to her face. "I don't think I understand."

"You remember what you said?" she asked.

"About what?"

"About negotiating. I wanted to help you, to understand your problems, and you were willing to negotiate."

"I remember." He wasn't sure he wanted to hear what she was about to say.

"Like you, I didn't want anyone to interfere

with my life. I fought them every step of the way. Then, eventually, I learned about the healing power, and I began to rebuild my life. I was very grateful that someone took charge and made me face my pain and learn to deal with it. Now I am repaying my debt."

"So you're beautiful now. Your mind works. You can still act, and any man would want you. I can attest to that. But I don't think you can do that for me."

They'd fixed her physical problems with laser surgery, but she was still injured in a way that no one could see. Joe's problems were equally grave; even if she succeeded in turning his mental state around, she had no answer for his bodily pain.

She sighed. He was right. She couldn't give him a good throwing arm and legs that would run. She couldn't restore his ability to play ball. Joe thought nobody needed him, and that, she suddenly understood, was the key. He had to have value. Somebody had to need something he could give. But what?

Then she knew. The answer had been there from the first. She had to make him believe that *she* needed *him*. Dare she tell him the truth? What was more uncertain was, could she get past her own fear?

What would Mac say? Or had he had this in mind from the beginning? Could the final step in her restoration be the solution to Joe's future?

It wasn't until dinner that evening that she found the courage to try.

"Joe, I have a proposition for you. Please listen."

The urgency in her voice captured all of Joe's attention. "I'm listening," he said.

"This is going to be hard to say. I don't even know if I can."

"Tell me, Annie."

"My body healed. My memory prior to that night came back, but I chose not to return to acting. Not yet—maybe not ever."

"Am I'm supposed to ask why?"

She swallowed hard and hoped he would believe what she was about to say. "I read a case study about you in my—the place where I've been undergoing rehabilitation. It was written by a man who does research on people who are good candidates to end their lives."

Joe was stunned. Somebody had written about him. Somebody knew how close he'd come to— "My problems are private. How dare somebody snoop into my private life?"

"It wasn't for publication. It was more in the nature of therapy, examples for a support group. I didn't ask for you, Joe, but when I read about you I knew that we were kindred spirits. We were both alone. We'd both turned our backs on life for different reasons."

He stood up abruptly, shoving the table with such force that the dishes rattled. "I was right in the first place, you're some kind of cult member. No thanks, babe, I'm not joining any group."

"Neither am I, Joe. I refused to admit it until now, but I'm not fully recovered. You may be my last chance. I need your help. You can decide whether or not you're willing to accept mine."

"What in hell could you possibly need from me?"

The question was there. What could she say to reach him that would make him accept her? How could she voice the secret that even Mac didn't discuss with her? There was a long, starkly powerful moment before she bared her soul and answered, "Sex."

"What?" He shook his head. Not in his worst alcohol-induced nightmares had he ever encountered a live sensual illusion that took his breath away and left him incapable of rational thought even when he was sober. "Did you say sex?"

"I did. Please, this isn't easy, Joe. I—my body needs your body. Something happened to me that night. My face wasn't the only part of my body the man hurt. Since then I can't—I mean I've never been able to . . . be with a man."

Joe took a step away, rubbing the same spot on his shoulder that she'd touched the first night. "This is pretty heavy stuff you're throwing around, lady. You just drop in out of the blue to save my lousy butt. That didn't make any sense, but this . . . ? You're asking me to—"

"That wasn't why I came. In fact, intimacy was

the last thing on my mind. But even you know that there is something between us."

Joe couldn't put her request into words. "What in hell makes you think that I have anything to offer you? I'm no therapist. I can't even deal with my own problems."

She couldn't turn back now. "That's what I thought too. Remember, you're at the same place now that I was when I realized I was still alive, but I'd lost any reason to care. Don't you see? In spite of everything, you've become my reason."

"Sorry, Goldy. This is too weird. I take back what I said about this being a nice way to start off the new year. I think we'd better rethink our plans."

She wasn't Annie anymore. He was trying to distance himself from her, from the enormity of the proposal she'd presented. She didn't blame him; the whole idea scared the hell out of her as well. Even so, she knew that for the first time she'd opened herself up to the truth.

Annie took a step forward, reached out, and touched his shoulder, allowing her hand to rest on his. Their chins were almost touching.

"Please, Joe. Don't send me away. Not yet. I promise I'm not crazy, and I'm not going to hurt you. We can help each other."

"I don't think so." He couldn't believe that he was turning down the most beautiful woman who'd ever offered herself to him. What in hell was he thinking of?

Of her—of the other people he'd cared about. The three people who'd meant the most to him in life had depended on him and they were gone.

Close was personal. Need was caring, and that hurt.

Sex was casual. It had to be.

But sex with Annie would never be a casual act. He felt Annie's pain—shared it. If he became personally involved in her life, he'd guarantee her the kind of pain in which he himself was trapped.

Annie watched the emtions flit across his face. She knew it was now or never. She could make it work or her honesty would end it all. If she failed, she was truly back to the same spot Joe was in now. There would be no future for either of them and they'd both attempted to eradicate the past.

Could she do what she had to? Could she divorce herself from personal involvement and play the part, be an actress if not a woman? Slyly, she reached up, cupped her hand across the back of his head, and pulled him down, closing her eyes and pressing her lips against his.

Joe didn't fight her. He seemed to be in shock, then slowly, not at all the way she'd expected, he seemed to relax and accept the tentative touch of her lips against his. After a second she felt the soft heat begin to flicker inside her. As if she were in a frame-by-frame, slow-motion viewer, she let herself give in to the need. Joe groaned. Only when he moved to pull her into his arms did the reality of what she was attempting release the fear.

She felt as if she were standing on the edge of a cliff, dizzy from the view below, her legs weak and ready to collapse. She tried to pull away, but if she didn't let him hold her up, she'd surely fall.

Fired by her kiss, Joe forgot all his reservations and responded like a normal male caught up in hot desire. Annie began to tremble—from fear or from need, she couldn't be certain—but as her anxiety grew Joe seemed to understand. He let his lips move to her cheek, whispering soft words as he relaxed his grip.

"Think, Joe," he was saying. "She told you that some crazy man did awful things to her. She hasn't been with a man since. But she trusts you. She needs you to help her. Do something right, Joe. For once, do something right."

Annie didn't have to be told that he was drawing on every ounce of self-control he could muster as he made space between them again.

"Take a deep breath, Annie. Nice and easy, as if you were down by the lake and didn't want to frighten the geese."

Automatically, almost as if she were standing outside herself, she followed his directions.

"Now, Annie, I'm going to put my arms back around you, gently, loosely. You can step away at any time. Just like when you were a very little girl and your mother comforted you."

"My mother never comforted me."

"Never? Not even when you were very small?" He started moving his arms around her, caressing her shoulders, her neck. "She must have when she fed you. Remember?"

A fleeting memory came to her, just a momentary glimpse of a woman with brown hair and thin arms lifting a small child into her lap. "Yes, I remember."

"And you were safe, weren't you? Not forever, but for a while." He pulled her a bit closer, and her resistance began to melt. In that moment he felt a tiny flicker of hope spring to life. Just this once he could give something back. Just once someone close to him wouldn't feel pain.

"It's all right, Annie, I'd never hurt you. I know what it is to be hurt, to hurt someone else. I may be a loser, Annie, but I promise you here and now that I'll never hurt you. Just like the geese, Annie, when one gets tired, it falls back and another takes the lead. We'll just hold each other, Annie. Help each other heal."

Suddenly she slumped against him, feeling the fear float away as she leaned her head on his shoulder. They stood for a long time, not speaking, not moving. Then he took her hand and led her toward the living room.

Once she sat down, he walked a few steps away. "Thank you, Annie, for offering yourself to me. But I could never take advantage of you."

"Why not?"

"For a lot of reasons, but mostly because you deserve better."

"I don't deserve anything at all, Joe. I may not

have learned anything else, but I know that to whom much is given, much is expected in return. I was a taker."

"A taker doesn't give back, Annie. You came to help me."

"But I failed you, Joe. I haven't helped you find a goal." She lifted moisture-laden eyes. "I'm impractical. I never look before I leap. And I'm a failure as a woman."

Joe glanced down at his body and let out a wry laugh. "My darling Annie, you may have failed at a lot of things, but you're no failure as a woman. You just need to let someone else shoulder part of the burden."

Could she do this, let Joe hold her? Forcing herself to think about the geese, she was able to relax, at least temporarily. Then, as she released her control, a hunger began to grow. Beginning deep inside her, it burned brighter and brighter. Joe, dear Joe, allowing her to see that her life need not be a lonely one.

Without being aware that she was about to do so, she stood and whispered, "Kiss me again, Joe. Please."

In the secret part of Annie's mind she was shocked at her request. That had been the last thing she'd ever have believed she'd say, the last thing she'd ever thought her body would have yearned for. The last thing she'd have considered. And yet, now, with no issue of a threat the need was there.

Annie knew that this whole situation was fraught with mistakes and the potential for disaster; still, her arms slid around his neck. "Joe?"

"To hell with reason," he growled, and pulled her into his arms.

Her breasts tingled where they touched his chest. "Joe—"

The telephone rang.

"No." Joe groaned, pulling his lips away from hers, clasping her bottom and pressing it against his arousal. "This only happens in a bad movie. Ignore it, Annie. Let the answering machine get it."

But the moment was shattered, and Annie's panic returned with the intrusion of a male voice. "Joe! Joe, answer this phone. This is Ace. I'm in the hospital, old buddy, and they won't let me out unless somebody comes for me. I need you to come get me."

Annie had backed up until she was standing against the wall, her breath thready, her eyes wide with fear. She'd wanted Joe to think that she needed him, and just for a minute she had. Oh, Lordy, she had. But the need was too fragile. It didn't last. She should have known better. Maybe she'd even made things worse—not for Joe, but for her.

"Joe!" the caller yelled out. "If you're there, wake up. I'm in the Kennestone Hospital Emergency Room in Cobb County. I've totaled my car, and I need a ride home. I've bailed you out enough times, turkey. It's your turn to return the favor."

Annie forced herself to walk to the phone and pick it up. "He'll be there, Ace. Joe will be there as soon as he can."

She hung up and faced Joe. "Go get him, Joe. We'll worry about our problems later. I may have blown my assignment, but you're not going to let your friend down. Helping others is a big step toward reclamation."

"Reclamation isn't exactly what I was going for."

Annie had sworn once that she'd never go to a hospital again. If she died, she'd do it under her own roof. If somebody else died, they could do it without her. Then she took a good look at Joe and saw the same reluctance on his face. Of course. Hospitals were the end of the line for Joe too. He'd lost his parents, then his body started to go. This wasn't going to be easy for either of them.

Annie took a deep breath. Being rushed to an emergency room was another part of her past she'd yet to face. How could she help Joe turn himself around if she couldn't turn her own self around?

She made up her mind. "I'll go with you, Joe."

When she headed toward the door, Joe, frustrated and silent, followed her. An unwanted mercy mission to the hospital wasn't his only problem. Helping Ace might be good for his soul, but every other part of him was screaming for another kind of release. What he needed from Annie now wasn't unselfish companionship.

What he needed was Annie's body. Damn his selfishness! He was just like the man in Annie's past. Joe Armstrong was turning Annie into his personal fantasy, and she knew it. He could see it in her eyes.

SIX

Just as Annie feared, the emergency room brought back jolting memories of the night of terror that had changed her life forever. Except this time she felt as if she were watching the scene unfold from some far-off place. There was no pain and no horror, just a feeling of total fear.

She'd expected to feel uneasy. On the way, she'd psyched herself into dealing with the problem as if it were a scene from her soap opera. But this was not the same. The sick and injured people sprawled in the seats weren't extras. The uniformed staff members and doctors weren't actors scurrying back and forth. Even her experience dealing with the teen who had been involved in the motorcycle accident hadn't prepared her, for he'd already been in therapy when she'd stepped in.

There'd been, it seemed, an accidental shooting, and as she watched the paramedics cope with the victim, all the pain came rushing back. The flash of a camera went off, and Annie ducked her face into Joe's shoulder.

"Annie—Annie, are you okay?" Joe's voice cut through the memories. "Take a deep breath." As she followed his directions a cold tremble started at the spot behind her knees, a reaction by which she measured her emotional response to any crisis.

The photographer who'd been her shadow for so long wasn't there in this hospital. This wasn't the place where Annie had been brought bleeding and screaming, her body invaded and her face destroyed, but it was just as real. This time, however, someone was holding her, taking on part of her anxiety.

"Don't fall out on me, darling. I don't understand why Ace called me, but we'll get him and go," Joe said, taking her arm and drawing her close as if he were protecting her.

Beneath his sheltering gesture, Annie could feel his rapid heartbeat. If she hadn't been there, she sensed that Joe would have been fighting demons of his own.

"All he had to do," Joe went on, "was call the coach and he'd have been out of this place."

Annie didn't answer. She'd thought she had her feelings under control. She didn't.

Joe squeezed her even closer as he skirted around a woman with a child. "Anybody on the team would have come. Hell, a stranger would jump at the chance to come to Ace Young's rescue."

Matching her steps to his, Annie leaned against him, instinctively drawing strength from the way he moved them along, sheltering her as if it were the most natural thing in the world.

"I'm sorry to spoil your evening, darling," he said.

It was the *darling* that cut through her terror and pulled her from her past to Joe's present. She hadn't expected his concern. Every painful personal memory she'd been fighting fell away, and she was completely focused on this man's problem instead of her own.

Ace was Joe's friend, and Joe was forcing himself to help, to be a kind of retriever. Not quite the same as what she'd had in mind for her charge, but it was a start.

"You don't suppose he's hurt bad, do you, Annie?"

"I doubt it. They wouldn't release him." Though, from the tales she'd read about Joe and his party-animal buddies, she thought that Ace might have called Joe because he wanted to keep the incident out of the papers. He'd be more willing to take a chance on Joe's understanding than anyone else.

"Maybe he's gotten himself into something really serious," Joe observed, a frown furrowing his forehead. He came to a stop at the information counter and waited while the receptionist spoke on the phone.

"Hospitals," he growled, glancing around the room. "They all look alike, don't they?"

Annie didn't try to hide her shudder. "I don't know about all of them, but I'm well acquainted with the pain and suffering they embrace. That's all the same."

Joe turned, understanding flashing across his face. "Oh, Annie, I'm sorry I dragged you along. I didn't think about how it would affect you."

"Hey, I'm okay. Hospitals are where people save lives."

"But they don't save everybody, do they?"

The consternation that swept across his face told her he was remembering the same kind of pain. He was remembering what happened to his parents.

This time when he put his arm around her she didn't tighten up. Touching must have been a part of Joe before he withdrew from contact with the outside world. It soothed, consoled. He was reassuring himself by touching her. She wondered if he'd realized what he was doing. Then, as if a voice spoke to her inside her mind, she knew the answer was no. Annie slipped her arm around his waist and felt a responding shudder of acceptance.

"Do you think Ace will mind that you brought me along?"

"I don't think Ace will mind. Besides, you're the one who answered the phone, so he already knows there's a woman in my life."

The hospital employee hung up the phone and

directed them to a small cubicle down the hall where the patient was waiting for assistance in leaving the hospital.

There's a woman in my life. Ordinary words casually spoken. But giving voice to the situation gave Joe a curious kind of satisfaction. In every other crisis in his adult life he'd gone solo.

This time he had Annie.

Ace was sitting on the side of the bed as they entered the curtained-off room. His face was bandaged, and as he stood he almost stumbled. "Thanks for coming, old buddy. I would have called my wife, but she's expecting, and I didn't want to worry her."

And this won't? Annie wanted to say.

"No problem," Joe repeated mechanically.

"I told those nurses that I could manage, but they wouldn't release me until I could find a guardian angel to claim me." The injured man caught sight of Annie and his face registered surprise. "Hey, I think this one will do real well."

"Ace, this is Annie." Joe moved his arm from her waist and slid it possessively across her shoulders.

Ace looked curiously at Joe and back at Annie before nodding. "Pleased to meet you, angel. Though I don't know why you'd pick this dude when I'm available."

"Maybe because you're married, Ace," Joe said, his voice almost cross. "Because your wife's having a baby. That kind of thing matters to some women."

"How badly are you hurt, Ace?" Annie intervened.

"Bad enough to get excused from practice tomorrow but not bad enough to be benched." Ace picked up his jacket. "Let's get out of here."

"What about your car?" Joe asked as he caught the fading smell of alcohol that pinpointed Ace's problem even if he didn't want to mention it.

"Don't ask," Ace countered.

"The cops?"

"I got lucky. Accident happened on private property and the officer was a fan. I hope you brought a limo. I need to lie down bad."

Joe gave a laugh of disbelief. "No limo, Ace. Just the Jeep. But you can have the whole backseat. Are you already checked out?"

"Right after I called you." As if she'd been waiting, a nurse appeared with a wheelchair. "Let's go, sweet thing."

"I'll get the Jeep." Joe jogged down the hall and disappeared from sight, leaving Annie to follow the nurse and Ace to the curb. Moments later Joe pulled up, jumped out, and opened the passenger door for Ace to get in. As if she'd done it a thousand times, Annie climbed in the front.

"Where do you want to go, Ace?"

"Go? Back to UGA. No, further back, high school maybe. Things were much simpler then. Life sucks, Joe."

Joe knew this wasn't fun-and-games talk. This was stark truth. "You're right about that, Ace. But believe me, it won't work. There ain't no going back. You or somebody you care about gets penalized for going the wrong way."

After a moment Ace forced himself to sit up, slapped his knee, and whistled, trying unsuccessfully to recapture the party spirit he'd lost. "You're right, Joe. Life is a bitch and then you die. Let's motor on over to the End Zone Bar and Grill and have a private little party."

"Not tonight, Ace," Joe said, finding Annie's worried face in the dark. "Annie and I have to get back home."

"Home! You and Annie? So it's like that, huh? Where'd you find an angel who'd take on a sinner like you?"

"I didn't. She found me. And I'm taking you home, Ace, where you belong."

Ace mumbled something, then leaned his head back against the seat and let out a deep sigh of resignation. "All is lost. Even old Joe has turned into a party pooper."

When they reached Ace's house he was snoring loudly. They had to wake his very pregnant wife, Lois, who seemed embarrassed. By the time they hussled Ace inside, Joe was ready to get away from the look of pain in her eyes. He'd had a few friends help bring him home in the past, but there hadn't been a wife to see his shame.

"We don't know where his car is," Annie was

explaining to her. "I'm sure he was ashamed over what happened; that's why he called Joe instead of you."

Then the two women turned away and the rest of the conversation was in furtive whispers. Joe couldn't be certain, but he thought that Ace's wife nodded as Annie gave her a hug of encouragement before they left.

"What's wrong with your friend?" Annie asked as they drove away. "Why is he drinking like that?"

"Nothing that a pair of young legs couldn't fix," Joe defended. "It happens to us, Annie. We all find our own way to hide. The drinking keeps you from having to face the truth—that your body gets old before you're ready for it."

"Drinking isn't going to help," she said without censure, "but it's easy to think it will."

Joe left the city and headed north toward his house, the effect of Ace's problem weighing heavily on his mind. "I don't know why he called me. I'm the last person on earth who can help him."

Annie leaned over and laid her hand on his thigh. "You're wrong, Joe. You're the first one who can. You've been there. You understand."

Joe swore. "*Been* there? Look, Annie, let's don't fool ourselves here. I'm still only one golden retriever away from where he is. If you weren't burning my leg with your touch, I'd be turning around and heading for the End Zone and the other losers who are already there."

"But you aren't," she said confidently.

He reached out and pulled her as close as he could in the awkward confines of the vehicle. "Get close to me, Annie." His voice was so gravelly that she could barely hear it. "Make me believe that I'm different."

"You are, Joe." She planted a hesitant kiss on his cheek, then reached across the gear shift so that she could move her left hand from his thigh and slide it behind his neck.

"For how long?"

"For now, one step at a time. Rehabilitation and motivation. Remember?"

He gave a satisfied chuckle. "You know, if I didn't know this was happening, I'd think I was dreaming. Ace wasn't so wrong, you know. I'd go back to high school in a minute if you were there. Things weren't screwed up then."

"For you maybe. I like where I am right now."

Joe smiled, reached out, took her right hand, and put it on his thigh. He had to reposition his leg so that she wouldn't feel how much he was responding to her touch. "I'm glad."

"I wouldn't go back for anything."

Annie's body stiffened almost imperceptibly when she mentioned going back. Joe felt it and sensed her resistance. He had a burning need to know why. Surely life couldn't be unkind to a beautiful, giving woman like Annie.

"I understand about losing your parents, Annie. And I understand what happened later. But was there never a time in your life when you didn't have a worry in the world except whether or not you'd get a zit on your face the day of a big date?"

Annie gave a bitter laugh. "Big date? Listen, Joe. There were no dates for Annie Calloway, big or small. My stepmother didn't allow me to go out during the week, and I worked every Friday and Saturday night of my entire high-school career."

She turned away, planting her elbow on the door and letting her hand slide back down to his thigh and stay there, almost as if she'd forgotten about it.

"What kind of work, Annie?"

"The worst possible place to build a reputation—in the local bus-station grill. My mama ran the café, kept it open twenty-four hours a day, seven days a week. She had to, to make a living. And I had to work there, if I wanted to live with her. I didn't, but until I had my diploma I couldn't leave. So . . . I survived."

"Didn't she like you?"

"Like me? I don't know. Maybe, under different circumstances. But what woman wants the man she loves to desert her and leave his kid behind? I felt as if she was punishing me because she couldn't punish him."

Joe released the gear and caught Annie's hand in his. He pulled it over and planted a kiss on her palm. "We both survived, I guess. Think it was because we needed to find each other?"

Her stomach rolled over. Joe threaded his fingers between hers, working them in and out, lifting her hand up and down. For a moment she was moving with him, until she recognized the suggestive motions and pulled her hand away.

"Maybe. Maybe it was," she whispered, though she knew in her heart that Joe Armstrong would never have taken out a girl who worked in the busstation grill. Annise, the actress and model maybe, but not Annie Calloway.

Joe drove the Jeep into the garage, led Annie up the steps into the house, and closed the door behind them. He waited there in the dark. "Now, Annie," he said, "where were we when the phone rang?"

"We were—were—"

"Kissing each other good night," he finished, touching his forehead to hers. "Thank you, Annie, for making me go, for going with me. If you hadn't been here, I'd never have done it."

"Why? Surely Ace would have done the same for you?"

"I never asked anybody to help me, Annie. I never trusted anybody but— People will let you down, Annie."

Annie wondered who'd let Joe down. Nothing in his file suggested that he'd been betrayed by anybody, unless he was thinking about his parents. But that didn't feel right. Joe was still wrestling with whatever or whoever abused his trust.

She needed to move away, but any movement would stop Joe's thought process. Though he'd been forced, he was putting someone else's needs above his own. Ace's call was a small thing, but it was the beginning of the kind of redirection of his life that she'd hoped for.

Now if her knees would stop registering her Joe response, she'd get through being so close to him.

Keep your mind focused on Joe's recovery, she told herself as Joe's lips brushed her face and cheeks, searing her with heat. She was having trouble with the sensitivity of her skin. It hadn't been this way before, even when the man she'd planned to marry had touched her.

Joe Armstrong overwhelmed her so easily, closing out all reason and control before she realized what was happening. He simply erased her defenses with his touch and her resolutions with his kisses. This wasn't supposed to be happening. She shouldn't want to touch him in return, but she did, rimming his earlobes, running her fingers down the tightly corded veins in his neck and inside his zippered sweatshirt.

She felt his bare skin and would have gasped had Joe's lips not found hers and covered them. His skin was warm, as if he, too, were burning. No man's skin could feel this hot to the touch, she thought. But it did, and it seemed to ripple beneath her fingertips, drawing her hands farther inside the shirt.

Annie knew she ought to push him away. She could feel Mac's censure nudging at her conscience as Joe tangled his fingers in her hair and pulled her head back. Mentally she directed Mac to go away as

Joe rained little kisses down her face and into the V between her breasts.

When had he unbuttoned her blouse and freed her breasts? She felt as if she were being turned inside out. Lips claimed, teased, and fired. Fingers caressed and sketched waves of heat across her skin. And it all felt so right.

Then Joe groaned, reached down, and clasped her bottom, pulling her into his full erection and moving himself against her. Every flicker of heat in Annie's body died an icy death. She jerked herself away, crying out in terror.

"No! Don't touch me!" The words tumbled out, and she couldn't stop them. "Don't ever touch me like that!" She whirled around and fled up the stairs, reaching the bathroom and slamming and locking the door. She collapsed onto the toilet seat and leaned forward, trying desperately to draw air into her lungs.

"Ohhhhh nooooo," she moaned, over and over while she swallowed back the lump of horror in her throat. What had she done? How had she let that happen?

Poor Joe. He must think she was loony. He couldn't be blamed for what happened. He didn't understand. She hadn't either. For Joe was the first man who'd gotten close to her. *Oh, Mac. I've blown it. You should never have sent me. I can't even help myself. Why did you think I could help someone else? I'm no better off than he is.*

Then she heard the creak of the stairs as Joe

climbed them. She hushed and moved to the door. If he forced it open, she'd simply walk out, go to the phone, and call a cab.

But he didn't try to open the door. Instead, he leaned against it. She could feel his presence on the other side, almost as vividly as if she was touching him. She could almost hear him breathe.

"I'm sorry, Annie," he whispered. "I didn't mean to frighten you. Please forgive me. I'm a selfish bastard, thinking only of myself."

"It isn't your fault, Joe."

"But it is. You made me feel so good, so powerful, something I've needed for so long. I never thought I'd feel it again. I was totally out of control, and I overwhelmed you without a thought."

"You don't understand, Joe," she said in a low voice. "You're such a physical man. I thought that I could use that to make you want me to stay. But it backfired. I wanted it—you. I've been fooling myself for a long time. I need to feel desire for a man, but I can't get beyond the wanting. Even when I feel desire, I can't go through with it. If I ever thought I could, what happened tells me I was wrong."

"Ah, Annie. I don't believe that. I'll admit I don't know much about how women feel after . . . after being attacked, but one thing I do know. I don't want you to go."

Annie listened to his words. Could she trust him? Could she trust herself? So far she hadn't managed to get Joe to commit permanently to any kind of action that would give him purpose in life. Everything had somehow focused on her, in a way she didn't understand.

"Can we talk about this, Annie?"

"No, not yet. I can't, Joe. I'm supposed to be helping you and I'm not. I'd better go before I make things worse for both of us."

"Go?" Joe felt a stab of pain shoot through him. He slammed his fist against the door and swore. This was what he'd wanted, what he'd feared. Somehow he'd messed up everything and everybody he'd cared about. And he was doing it again.

"Yes, please let me go."

"Hell no! You stopped me from driving off a mountain, and you're not walking out on me now. Haven't you heard? When you save a life, it belongs to you. I'm yours, darling. You said you were my last train to redemption, and I'm climbing on. You're stuck with me."

"No, Joe. I'm sorry."

"I won't accept that. I don't know who sent you, but he knew what he was doing. I'll prove it to you. You just wait right here. I'll be back."

Annie stilled her breathing and listened to the sound of his footsteps as he dashed down the stairs. A door opened and closed.

Then a familiar sound drew her to the window. It was coming from below the stoop at the front door. She shook her head in disbelief, then raised the window. "What are you doing out there, Joe?"

"Remember Jimmy Stewart and the bridge. Can you hear my bell?"

She couldn't stop herself from smiling. In the midst of trauma, of pain, of uncertainty, she could clearly hear the distinct sound of a bell, tiny but insistent.

"You remember," he was shouting. "When an angel gets her wings, a bell rings."

"Dear Joe," she whispered. "I wish it were that easy."

"Let me in, Annie," Joe called out. "Please."

"You're a fool, Annie Calloway!" she said as she opened the bathroom door.

"Hurry," Joe said as he waited outside, shaking the sleigh-bell ornament from the Christmas tree. "Let me in. The door locked behind me."

She ought not to move, she knew it as she opened her door. "Even worse than being a fool, you're a failure," she said as she walked down the stairs. "You're doing just what Mac told you not to do—get involved personally."

"Annie, help me," he called pitifully as he heard the knob turn.

She gave up. "I'm only doing this because of Ace. He needs you, Joe. You have to believe that there are people who need you."

"And there are people who need you, Annie."

She opened the door and looked into the haunted face of the man she'd been sent to save. She felt a rip in her heart and the pain welled up in her as they looked at each other.

"You know this could be the end of both of us, Joe Armstrong."

"Or the beginning."

"All right, Joe. We'll try. We'll start over. I don't know if we can make it work, but I promised someone important to me that I'd try. I still have four more days to go."

"Look around you, Annie. At the end of two days the Big Guy had only gotten as far as the planet, the ocean, day and night. I'd say four days ought to be plenty of time for you."

"You think so?"

"Besides, we haven't played Scrabble yet."

SEVEN

The next morning a very serious Joe came to the kitchen and sat down, settling his hands on the breakfast table as if he were about to make a pronouncement. "Good morning, Goldy. What may I have for breakfast?"

Goldy? "What would you like?" she asked. She'd been prepared for anything from teasing to awkwardness to a battle, even half looking forward to it. But half the fun of working with Joe was his scrappy manner, his determination that she wouldn't get to him.

He picked up the newspaper and glanced at the headlines. "Whatever you say. I'm clay ready to be molded, just like you wanted."

But this Joe wasn't what she wanted. He was resigned, as though he was playing out a role. "What I want is the Joe I knew last night, the one who cared about me, about Ace and his wife. Where did he go?"

"He's behaving himself. He's been sanitized, Goldy. Give him your best shot."

Goldy again. Annie felt anger swell up inside her. "I didn't think you were a coward, Joe Armstrong, but you are."

"And you aren't? What's the difference in your being ready to bolt every second and what I'm doing?"

"You don't understand," she stammered. "I—I'm not the one in danger of being lost forever."

He folded the paper and laid it down. "What does it take to make us even?"

That stopped her for a moment. She didn't know the answer. But she had to be honest if she were to have any chance of succeeding.

"Doesn't matter," he observed. "Just lay it out. Or," he amended, standing up again, "tell me what you want me to do. I promised you last night I'd be a good soldier, and I will."

He couldn't tell her that the only way he could keep his word and not touch her was to put distance between them. He noted her confusion, but he couldn't think of a way to stop it without putting his vow at risk.

"What I want you to do is to stop looking as if you think the world as we know it is ending as we speak." Her voice had turned sharp and she didn't know why. This wasn't the way the day was supposed to start.

Joe ran his fingers through his hair and let out a deep breath. "Sorry, Annie. I guess I just didn't sleep well. I'm not used to someone being in the house. Is there coffee?"

"There's coffee and wheat toast and fruit." She pushed the bread down in the toaster, then lifted the pot and turned to the table, filling both cups.

"Sounds fine. You look very nice this morning," he said in a belated attempt at making the morning seem normal. That was going to be hard. Nothing was normal, hadn't been since Annie had appeared at his door.

He hadn't been able to sleep. Hot showers hadn't helped, neither had cold showers. Pacing the confines of his room hadn't helped either. Finally he'd slipped down the stairs, and after finding Annie sleeping on the couch, he'd spent a good part of the night running along the highway, something his body highly resented now.

He'd been amused to find that she'd slept with the light on in the kitchen, like a little girl afraid of the dark. She had cradled her face with her arm, and even with her eyes closed, she'd made his heart thud. He'd been tempted to touch her, lift her in his arms and take her upstairs to his bed where she'd be safe from harm.

His bed. *Where she'd be safe*. Who was he kidding? He didn't know what that crazy man had done to Annie, but whatever it was, he'd left her just as scarred as Joe was himself. Two beautiful people, both burned on the inside. But she'd found a way out, at least on the surface. He wondered how far she'd really come.

Thinking of how he'd watched her sleep, Joe decided "nice" was a lame description of the way she looked awake. Her eyes weren't just green; they were the color of grass, all fresh and new. She'd pulled her golden hair into a ponytail, and it left her face open to his scrutiny.

Annie brought the cream and sugar to the table. "You shaved. You look like a different person."

Joe stood there awkwardly. He'd told her he wouldn't touch her unless she asked, but he was having trouble making his arms remember that. He'd put the table between them, praying his legs wouldn't take off on their own and step over it.

As he'd run through the gray dawn Joe recognized that he'd spent little time with women who needed reassurance. He didn't know how to act after he'd scared the life out of her the night before. She might not understand his stoic manner, but it was the only thing keeping him from kissing her. Starting over was going to be hard after he'd felt her lips beneath his, her body against his. But her wary look across the table made him go slow.

"You think I'm a different person, Annie. Well, I'm not. Everything is still the same."

"I don't think so, Joe. Nothing ever stays the same, even when we want it to. We just have to find the direction we want to go in."

"So, Annie, the Retriever of Lost Souls is still on the job," he cracked. "Fine. Bring on the wheat toast and fruit. What happens after breakfast?"

She let out a sigh of relief, feeling the tremble behind her knees begin to recede. "We're going to talk. Then we're going to make some lists. Then we're going to make some decisions."

He picked up the cup, cradling it in his hand, and swirled the liquid around the edge. "At least you're still talking about *we*."

"Did you think that would change?"

"I didn't know."

The toast popped up. Annie caught both pieces and placed them on a saucer, handing it and a tub of butter to Joe before slapping two more pieces in for herself.

"Don't suppose we're having jelly?" he asked, lifting his brows.

"Absolutely not!" When she saw his pained expression, she couldn't help adding, "Not if you're going to dip our apples in caramel tonight."

"Caramel apples," he said softly, registering her impish tone. "You know, I never really had them. Oh, I had apples, of course, but dipping them in caramel would have been considered a luxury, and a Methodist minister does well to provide only the essentials."

Annie's toast was ready and she sat down across from Joe. "I know. I used to hate the café at the same time as I was filling my stomach with the left-overs."

"I guess I was lucky. I had plenty to eat. The congregation tried to make up for the low salary they paid my father by sharing whatever they had with us. I understood early on that being strong and healthy was my ticket out of Eufaula, and I never turned down food. But sometimes it was hard to accept that we were always dependent on others. I'm afraid I was a burden to my poor father."

Annie nodded. "I suppose. But having food didn't mean much to me. I might have felt differently if I'd been hungry. But back then I'd rather have had clothes or makeup and jewelry."

He looked at her curiously. "I suppose that would be pretty tough for a girl. A guy is either a jock, a brain, or a stud. A girl—how'd you get through it?"

"Not too well I'm afraid. I turned into an intellectual. Not a brain—a freethinker. I joined the drama club, wrote poetry, had deep philosophical discussions with the other great thinkers. People in the theater can be as weird as they like. Others expect it. I didn't wear any makeup or jewelry. My clothes—well, let's just say they were supposed to look decidedly original."

Joe took a long look at Annie. He couldn't picture her as a misfit. He could no longer picture her as a vamp on a soap opera either. She was just—just Annie. And he liked her a lot because he understood her. They were more alike than he wanted to think. As he tried to untangle his feelings she raised her eyes from her plate, caught his troubled expression, and smiled.

"What's the matter, Joe? Can't you see me as a wild child?"

"Now that I know you better, no. And I can't see you as an actress either. You're too soft, too gentle." When she winced he reached for something less personal. "What about me? Can you see me as a brain?"

She took a long, measuring look at the big blond athlete and shook her head. "Nope, 'fraid not. I'm sorry, but you're forever labeled as a jock."

He groaned and took a big swallow from the glass of orange juice beside his place. "And I was sure you were going to say stud. Guess I'll have to work on my image."

After a rocky beginning, the rest of the day went fine. Annie kept prodding Joe for some indication of a direction for what she called his soul service. In the manual it was called *direction of service for the purpose of restitution*. To Annie, it was all about reaching inside and finding your humanity.

Finally, around midafternoon, she leaned back in her chair and closed her eyes. "I give up, Joe. You don't have any hobbies, no interests other than sports, and no friends who aren't involved in football. That might be all right if you could use football to help others."

"I tried," he said seriously. "I applied for several coaching jobs and got turned down for all of them. Though I think the people who interviewed me were smart not to hire me at the time. I couldn't have told anybody else what to do because I couldn't even manage myself."

But it was himself Joe screwed up, his present and his future. It had started with a lie that even now was weighing him down with guilt. Joe Armstrong had always been honest. He'd always taken the pain with the praise. Except once, when he'd let confusion overrule his ethics.

"What about children?" Annie asked. "You could work with children."

"No good, Annie. I don't have the patience. Today's kids are too smart for their own good."

"Weren't you the same?"

"Yes—I mean no. After third grade I never had a smart mouth."

"What happened in third grade?"

"I met Mrs. Lacey. She was two years past retirement, stood four feet, two inches tall, and had a mean left hook. After a couple of rounds with some boxing gloves, we came to an understanding."

Annie tried to imagine a teacher boxing with a third grader and couldn't. "So you made your mouth behave to please her."

Joe grinned. "No, I discovered girls don't like a smart mouth either. Speaking of mouths, yours has a tiny little pucker at the corner. Did you know that?"

He had gone all day without touching her, and he couldn't stand it a minute longer. He leaned over and tilted her head toward the light coming through the window under the pretense of examining it more carefully.

Her breath made a fast exit, leaving her with a sensation so dizzying that she could hardly sit still. "No. I don't think I did."

"Football players learn all kinds of first-aid techniques," he confided. "I think I ought to take care of that pucker before it gets any worse."

He knew as soon as he did it that he shouldn't have touched her. But after a day of holding his need to touch in check, he'd gone as far as he could go.

Using Annie's physical response wasn't fair, but maybe he could get her to accept some simple, nonthreatening affection. Then he'd figure out a way to make her feel good about what was obviously happening between them.

He ran his finger across the top of her lips, teasing the corner as he studied it intently.

By the time she realized that he was about to do more, his lips were almost within kissing distance of hers.

"No, Joe," she whispered, trying to disguise her trembling. "You promised."

"Ah yes. I did. I got rid of my smart talk, but my mouth still has a mind of its own. What can I say?"

"Something physical," she said, without realizing how that sounded. "What I mean is, let's do something physical." Her explanation was getting worse. Feeling her face flame, she shoved herself away from the table. "I mean, let's go for a walk, work up an appetite for alfalfa sprouts."

"Good idea. I like physical. That's one thing I do well."

"Joe—"

"Sorry. It must be the idea of alfalfa sprouts," he said, pulling on his sweat jacket and zipping it. "I think they accelerate my wild urgings."

"I think it's the caramel. You know what too much sugar does to a person."

Joe stopped and looked at Annie, his lips quirking in spite of his determination to be cool. He didn't know why their conversation had turned silly, but it had and it felt good.

"You know we are making no progress, Joe," Annie began as they stepped outside. "By now I'd hoped to have helped you find a project that would give you something worthwhile to focus on."

The snow had disappeared from the road right away. Now it was gone from the pines and bare trees between the house and the lake. Annie stood for a moment, then started up the road past Joe's house.

In the silence she could hear the honking of geese. The crisp clean smell in the air made her feel new inside. She wished it were that easy, just to wake up to a new day that was clean and good.

"Annie, I know you're following orders and I'm certain that somebody somwhere must have worked all this out. But I wonder . . ."

"What?" She stopped and turned toward Joe.

He had to find a place to look other than at her mouth. It was soft and childlike, appealing to some gentleness, some faint stirring of goodness long past, altogether much too appealing.

Under his gaze she shivered slightly and closed her eyes as if someone had told her to make a wish and she was complying. For a moment he forgot what he was about to say and had to concentrate to recall their conversation.

"What was your project? Why did you have to find something to make you feel worthwhile?" he asked.

"Because I couldn't go back to the life I'd lived before. It wasn't just the attack, it was the lifestyle. It almost killed me. My body recovered, but my mind wasn't interested in anything. I needed—motivation." She turned and started back up the road.

Joe hurried to catch up to her. "And what was your motivation?"

"Mac thought that—"

"Wait a minute, who is Mac?"

"Mac's the man I work with, the man who helped me. He sent me to you."

Joe held up a low hanging branch and Annie ducked under it. "And who told your Mac that Joe Armstrong needed help?"

He waited as Annie took a second to answer. "I can't answer that, Joe. Nobody knows. I just know that if it hadn't been for Mac, I would be dead."

"So, go on. He sent you to me and . . . ?"

"He promised if I helped somebody whose life was as hopeless as mine, I'd see that there was hope for me."

"Damn! That's another heavy load you're putting on me."

Annie stopped and looked back. "Another?"

"Sure. First sex. Now therapy—if you don't reform me, there's no hope for you." If there was one thing he'd learned it was that Joe Armstrong was a jinx to anybody who depended on him. "And if you fail, are you going to find your own mountain road?"

"No. I may not be completely recovered, but I'm past eneding it all, Joe. You aren't the first client I've worked with."

That should have reassured him, but it didn't. He didn't want Annie depending on anyone else. "I see. So I'm just icing on the cake, so to speak."

"Not exactly."

"Then what exactly?"

"I'm not very good at this sort of thing. I have to help the client stand on his own. But I always get too involved, make it too personal. The outcome can't depend on my involvement, and so far it has."

Joe nodded his head, his smile broadening. "Involved. Hey, that's exactly what I had in mind, Annie. If I have to have a project, I've decided on one."

She was beginning to understand the way Joe's mind worked. When he was pulling away, she was Goldy. But when he relaxed and let her slip inside, she was Annie. Of course he couldn't admit to any genuine feelings, so he resorted to being flippant.

"You have? What?"

"You. My project is you. You said that you're a work in progress, that you aren't done yet."

His answer shouldn't have surprised her, but it did. "Don't be silly, Joe. This is serious. I'm not the one who is important. It's you. Helping you is my last chance. If I fail, I'll have to find something else to do with my life, and that could mean going back to the bus-station café."

"What about your acting?"

"The world's forgotten about me, remember? This isn't a television script where we can explain all this away by saying it was just a dream."

"Why not—it happens all the time."

"Sure, I've been suffering from amnesia for three years. I'll jump in the river and you can rescue me and the soap star Annise will come back to life."

"No! Don't joke about that!" His voice swept away the joking, bringing their nonsensical chatter to an abrupt stop. "Not about—"

Annie didn't know what she'd said, but she knew that whatever it was, she'd come close to touching the core of Joe's destructive behavior. She wished she had more knowledge, knew more about how to reach Joe, to help him.

"What did I say, Joe? What did I do?"

"You didn't do anything," he said, brushing past

her, his mouth set. "Just forget it. It was the thought of having something happen to you."

But that wasn't it, not totally. Annie knew it. "I'm sorry, Joe. I didn't mean to pry. I don't want to force you to share your pain unless you want to."

"I don't."

"Well, I won't give up," Annie said. "I owe my life to Mac, the man who sent me to you. He thinks that I can save you. I have to try, even if you don't understand."

"You're right. I quit trying to understand when I kissed you. I even quit hating sprouts and tofu." He stopped, chewed his lip for a minute, then asked, "About this Mac, is he CIA or something?"

"No. He's just a very private person."

"Look, why don't I go talk to him? There's no reason for him to give you a hard time just because I'm such a lost cause. *He* couldn't do any better."

Standing there in the middle of the road, with a sudden current of cold air sweeping past them, Annie was suddenly aware of the strong cut of Joe's chin. She could understand how facing him on the playing field would put fear in the heart of an opponent. With his sun-streaked brown hair and blue eyes, he looked like every girl's heartthrob. But Annie Calloway was in over her head, and she couldn't go forward or retreat. This was more than just Joe's survival, more than helping him find his way. Her own sense of self and of accomplishment were at stake.

Annie forced herself to respond. What had he

said? Oh yes, that Mac couldn't do better. "Oh, but you're wrong, Joe. Mac could do better. Mac is very powerful. He has ways that I don't begin to understand. He's—"

"I know. I already figured it out. Mac is either assistant to the big saint at the gate or the devil. Maybe you sold your soul to him and now he's after mine. Well, why not? Send for him, and maybe we'll work out a deal."

Annie gasped. "Don't make jokes."

"I'm not joking, darling. Yesterday I figured out that it doesn't matter what you really are. I'm willing to take my chances."

Annie's head was beginning to ache. "I don't understand what you mean. Figured out what? What do you think I am?"

"I thought, that first night, that you were an angel. If you're not an angel, then you have to be a witch. If you don't belong to a choir, you must belong to a coven. What I'm trying to figure out is whether you're good or bad. Nah—check that, I don't even care."

"That's it. I give up. I'm going back to the house and start supper. Rob will like my fare, even if you don't."

"Rob? What does my manager have to do with all this?"

"He called this morning while you were in the shower. He said he needed to talk to you, and I invited him to dinner."

"No way. I've already told Rob that I'm not

going to get involved in that park project. I'm no fund-raiser. I don't ask anybody for help."

"Park project?"

Damn, he'd done it now. After all the questions and prodding, he'd managed to remain totally neutral. Now, in one sentence, he'd given her what she'd spent hours looking for.

Joe Armstrong had given Annie Calloway a cause. He could see from the look in her eyes that that was all she needed. Well, once she found out about that dinner dance, she'd probably insist on his going.

Well, if she wanted to get herself all dressed up in that gold spandex dress and go with Rob to a fancy formal affair, she could do it. He certainly had no intention of watching her. Suppose somebody from the press was there, somebody who might recognize the superstar named Annise? He gave the matter some thought. No, that wouldn't happen, he decided. She said she didn't look the same. But she didn't have to. In that gold dress she'd be front-page news anyway.

He'd already changed his mind about the party.

Annie never exaggerated about her cooking. She knew that Rob would love it and she was right. After half an hour of conversation, Annie loved Rob too.

"This is great," Rob said as he finished up the

last bite of caramel-apple pie. "Where did you learn to cook like this?"

"I once worked in a restaurant," she said. "Keeping a cook was hard. It was strictly a matter of self-preservation."

"How on earth did Joe find someone like you?"

"He didn't. I found him."

"I'm her project," Joe offered. "She's on a mission to reclaim my lost soul and give me purpose in life." His voice was too sharp, and he felt bad as soon as he saw her wince.

Rob glanced at him with a puzzled expression. "Is this some kind of therapy? Did you finally decide to get yourself together?"

"Not me," Joe said lamely. "It's all her idea. *We're* finding an afterlife for an ex-ballplayer."

"Any suggestions?" Annie asked innocently, turning a frown to Joe and a smile of question to Rob.

"If Joe is serious, I might just have an idea."

"Don't say it, Rob. I do not intend to get involved in this project."

Annie stood up and began to clear the table. She'd waited all through the meal to find out what he'd meant before. "What is the project, Rob?"

"The Falcon team wives want to make the new downtown Olympic Park more user-friendly to the handicapped. They're mounting a fund-raising project."

"How nice. That certainly seems worthwhile." The project was commendable, but Annie couldn't see fund-raising as something Joe would feel passionate about on a permanent basis. Still, it was worth considering. Like the incident involving Ace, it was a step in the right direction.

Rob seemed to sense that Annie could be an influence on Joe. "They're kicking off the campaign with a Winter Ball, a formal dinner dance tomorrow night at the Waverly Hotel. Why don't you come with Joe? I have his tickets."

A public appearance—a ball. Could she do it? "I'd love to," she said quickly.

"Do what you like," Joe said just as quickly, "but I'm not going."

Rob looked at Joe for a moment, then pursed his lips and asked, "Don't suppose you'd go with me, Annie?"

"Of course I will." Annie's face lit up. "I have just the dress to wear. It's Joe's favorite. He loves the length." She reached for the pot. "Would you like coffee, Rob?"

Joe groaned. He'd seen it coming. He couldn't see any way out. Annie knew exactly what she was doing, backing him into a corner where he couldn't refuse. One look at her, and those horny studs would strut through his house like a flock of those geese following the lead bird. Annie was his, and what he felt was too fragile to be tested.

Rob responded, but not to the offer of coffee. "Do I hear you changing your mind, Joe?"

Joe shrugged. "Why should I? If Annie wants to

get involved with a bunch of do-gooders, it's her choice. I'll even let her go with you. Hell," he swore, and grabbed his jacket from the hook by the door, "I'll even spring for a limo for you."

The slam of the kitchen door echoed through the house.

Rob looked at Annie. "I don't know what he's so upset about, but I think you're getting to him."

"I hope so." She chewed on her lower lip, wondering whether or not to broach the subject, then decided that she didn't have enough time to hesitate. "Tell me about Ace."

"Well, he isn't my client, but I keep up with all the Falcons. He's had a pretty rough time. Injuries have kept him out of the game. Then they traded for a young kid who looks really good. Ace sees the handwriting on the wall."

"But I don't understand. All the players must know that the day will come when they can't play. Why aren't they better prepared?"

"I've thought a lot about that," Rob confided. "Take Joe. He spent his entire life either getting ready to play or playing ball. It was to take him out of a nothing little town and make him a star. And it did."

"But," she finished the story, "he never took any time along the way to prepare for life after football."

"That's right. And he isn't the only one. There are a few who set their sights on coaching. Some go into broadcasting. There are players who actually manage to get college degrees that give them some competency outside of football. But those are damned few."

"So they either go off quietly into the night, or they come apart."

"Something like that," Rob agreed.

Annie finished clearing the table and brought coffee cups, which she filled, then sat down. "I know Joe didn't get a degree. Is that why nobody wants him to coach?"

"A degree doesn't matter in the pros, but with the new eligibility regulations on the college level, the coaches have to set examples. There ought to be a professional program geared toward helping those who retire. Joe has so much to give if he could find a focus for his energy."

"Maybe we could do something, Rob. Help players like Joe and Ace."

"Sure, and maybe pigs could fly. You know what would happen if Joe even thought that somebody was feeling sorry for him? And he's no different from the rest. They know they need help, but they're too proud to ask."

For the next half hour Annie and Rob kicked around several ideas about how such a project could be started. But when Joe failed to return, Annie began to worry. After several glances at his watch, Rob stood and began making his excuses.

"Maybe I'll just leave. Joe can't have gone too

far since he's on foot. If you're serious about attending the festivities, call me tomorrow and I'll pick you up."

Distracted now, Annie only nodded. Where was Joe? Why had he disappeared?

Rob opened the front door, then stopped. "Tell you what, Annie. Why don't I just leave you the tickets. In case Joe changes his mind."

He laid them on the hall table and left through the front door. Annie reached for her jacket and went out the rear. Only because of the night-light in the back did she find the path down to the lake. If Joe wasn't there, she didn't know where to look.

She'd made the right choice. He was by the water, mangling a roll he'd apparently swiped from the stove on the way out.

"Are you going to give that to the ducks, or are you working on some kind of hand exercises?"

Joe looked down at the crumbs as if he hadn't known they were there, then threw them into the water. He put his hands on his hips and stood, back turned, unyielding as if he were daring her to intrude.

Annie looked for an innocent topic to broach. "You must really enjoy living on the lake in the summer. Picnics. Swimming. Boating."

"I never go in the water." His words were clipped and harsh.

She'd heard that same tone in his voice when she'd joked about returning to life after nearly drowning. "Why? Don't you swim? I'm pretty good at it. If we can find an indoor pool, I could teach you."

"This is as close as I get to the water—ever. Swimming could never be an option on your rehabilitation and motivation list." He left no room for argument in his voice.

Annie couldn't be sure whether he was afraid of the water, or was simply using the excuse to let her know she'd gone too far. "I'm sorry if I upset you tonight, Joe. I didn't mean to pressure you into doing something you don't want to do."

He let out a ragged sigh. "You didn't do anything wrong, Annie. I only blew up because I felt like such a heel for refusing to take you to the ball. It's just that since Jack died, I've had a hard time facing the boys."

"Jack?" This was a new name to Annie. "Who is Jack?"

"You mean that wasn't in your little black book on the life and times of Joe Armstrong? Jack was my roommate, my best friend, my running buddy."

Was she wrong in reading relief into his manner? He seemed glad that she didn't know about Jack. Maybe it was better if she professed her ignorance, though she didn't understand such an omission in Joe's file. She put her hand on his arm. "What happened to him?"

Joe turned around and faced her. It was too dark for him to see her expression and too late to take back the terrible secret he'd just shared. "You really don't know what happened?"

"No. I do seem to remember the name, something about an accident. But there were no details." It was coming back to her, the details. He'd been killed in a boating accident.

She thought Joe wasn't going to explain. For a long time he simply looked at her, then he moved back to a rock near the edge of the lake and leaned against it. "Jack was the brother I never had. When my mother and dad were killed, he was all I had."

"And he was killed?"

"Six months ago, in a boating accident, on this very lake."

"No wonder you don't swim here now. I'm sorry I brought it up. I didn't mean to make you hurt."

"The hurt never goes away, Annie. How can you forget something that horrible?"

"Accidents happen, Joe. You can't blame yourself."

"Of course I can. He shouldn't have been driving the boat. I knew he'd had too much to drink, and I let him. He drove the speedboat under the arena dock and hit his head. He's dead, and I killed him as surely as I'm standing here, Annie. Now you know it all."

"Oh, Joe."

"Don't feel sorry for me, Annie. And don't get close. The people who get close to me die, Annie. I can't live with that happening again."

He brushed past her and made his way back to the house, leaving her in the darkness. She felt the weight of the pain he carried around. Annie had never killed anybody. But she'd spent a year wishing that her assailant had killed her.

EIGHT

Day Four was a surprise. Joe was gone when Annie woke. He'd left the Scrabble Board open on the counter with two words spelled out. DON'T GO.

A second holder with seven letters on it had been left across the board. She studied the combination, then unscrambled Joe's word, forming the only possible combination: TOGETHER. She smiled at the way he'd used to communicate. It might be a game, but the message was real. But when the hours passed and he hadn't returned, she began to worry.

Annie finally called the one person who could possibly help. "Mac, what do you know about Joe's friend Jack?"

There was a silence and a ruffle of papers. "Not much. Jack was Joe's roommate on the road. He even bought a house across the lake from Joe. They were close friends, party animals, apparently."

"But Jack's dead. What happened?"

"The report just says a boating accident. He'd been drinking and drove his speedboat under the dock at a marina. He was killed. There's no obvious connection, but his death contributed to Joe's downward spiral. Everybody attributed Joe's deteriorating performance on the ball field to losing his favorite receiver. Then Joe began to lose confidence in himself. Why, is this important?"

"Yes, I think it is. Jack's death was even more traumatic than you know. Joe told me he knew Jack had been drinking and he let him drive the boat. He holds himself responsible for not stopping his friend."

"That explains a lot, Annie. His knees were already bad and his arm was losing its zip. Jack's death must have been the emotional straw that broke the camel's back. But his telling you is a good sign."

"Maybe," Annie agreed. "Maybe I shouldn't have pushed him away. Now he's gone."

"Pushed him away? What does that mean, Annie?"

"He kissed me, Mac, and I kissed him back. I know I'm not supposed to get close, but just for a moment I wanted him, Mac. I even offered him a bribe to cooperate."

"Is that what you want, Annie?"

"What I want? What do you mean? You know what happened to me and how far I've come. You warned me not to expect a normal life and I don't."

"No, Annie. I told you that the rest of your life is up to you. You're important to me. You've come a long way. Maybe Joe will have to help you find the rest of your way. Sometimes we don't know where we're going until we get there."

"You're not making any sense, Mac. Joe can't even find his own way. He sure can't help me. Even if he could, it wouldn't work. I got up this morning and he was gone."

"There must be something you can do, Annie," Mac argued. "What did you disagree about?"

"Attending a fund-raiser, a dinner dance."

"You want to go? Aren't you worried about being recognized?"

"No. After all, you've told me over and over that I'm a very different person. Sure, I've avoided the spotlight, but now, if it meant helping Joe, I'd go."

"Then do it."

"He refused. I've failed, Mac. Maybe you'd better send someone else."

"Don't get crazy, Annie. Just because Joe's disappeared doesn't mean that you aren't getting to him. Tell me more about the dance."

She told him about the project and the invitations left by Joe's manager, Rob. "I have a half a mind to go with Rob if Joe doesn't change his mind."

Mac laughed lightly. "I think you'll find the answer."

"Yeah. Sure," she told herself as Mac hung up,

"and if I could sprout angel wings, I'd find a mate and fly with the geese out back."

It was late afternoon when Joe finally returned, whistling a dance tune as he climbed the steps from the garage. At the top he stopped, stuck his head in the door, and called out, "Annie? Is it safe for me to come in?"

Annie let out a sigh of relief and lowered the sports magazine she was reading. "It's your house, Joe."

"Uh-oh! The lady is angry."

"Not angry, but she's counting. This is day four, or what's left of it, and I only have three more to go. Why did you run away?"

"I'm sorry if I worried you, but I had some thinking to do and some shopping." He stepped inside, carrying a large box wrapped and tied with a red bow.

Annie watched as he laid the box across her knees. His eyes were bright and clear, as blue as the sweater he was wearing and just as warm. He looked like a little boy who'd been shopping for a gift for his first girl. Now he was fidgeting—impatient, proud.

"What's this?" she asked.

"Open it and see."

Annie should have refused. She'd spent the day telling herself to get back on track; that her assignment was a business arrangement. Presents were personal. Still, she couldn't resist the hint of mischief in Joe's eyes. If this gift was a peace offering, she'd take it.

Sliding the bow off, she peeled away the shiny white paper and caught the edges of the top, lifting it to reveal a layer of white tissue.

"What in the world?" she said, studying it as though she were trying to guess what was beneath the paper.

Joe's patience had run out. She could see that he couldn't stand it any longer. He pushed through the paper and pulled out a white fur coat—a very long fur coat. Before Annie could comment, Joe had pulled her to her feet and was threading her arms into the sleeves.

"Now you'll look like one of the snowflakes from the *Nutcracker*, all gold and white."

"Fur?" was all she could manage.

"Not real, Annie. I knew you wouldn't wear that. This is a very expensive fake."

"But I can't accept this, Joe."

"Why not?"

"It's against the rules."

"Rules. There are too many rules in this world, and I made a vow long ago to break one of them every day for the rest of my life. This is today's."

Annie rubbed her chin against the soft nap of the fur. She wasn't certain how to respond. Joe had obviously bought it for her to wear to the ball. Did that mean he was going to accompany her?

Was that what she wanted?

The answer was yes. It had been a long time since she'd ventured out in public. It was time. And this event would likely guarantee that she'd be on display. But she wanted to go with Joe, and he'd just given her the weapon. "Thank you, Joe. I'm not supposed to do this, but I will—if you'll do something for me. Fair enough?"

Joe nodded reluctantly.

"Fine, I'll accept the fur if you'll escort me to the ball. And that's my broken rule for today. I'm not sure I can face a crowd without you."

"I have a confession. I don't dance, Annie."

"I'll teach you. We have time." She held out her arms.

Joe took a step forward, then glanced ruefully at his watch. "No point in that Annie. I couldn't go if I wanted to. I don't have a tux. But I would enjoy a short session of swaying to the music."

"I have a confession, too, Joe. I had Rob rent a tux for you and send it over. It's in your room."

He'd told himself all day that he'd offer her the coat as payment for what she'd attempted to do for him. She meant well and she ought to be rewarded. Then he'd explain that under the circumstances, she could see why he was not worth her efforts. He was a lost soul and even she couldn't redeem him. In order to be saved, he had to want to be forgiven, and his guilt was much too great.

Then he surprised himself by smiling. "That sure of me, were you?"

"No, but I was hoping." She crossed her arms

over her chest and squeezed them against her. "Please, Joe."

He wanted to go, to be with her. Could he face his teammates and the coach? "Do you like the coat?"

"It's lovely. But it's far too expensive, and"— she glanced down at her ankles where the coat touched—"maybe just a tad too long?"

"No, it's not too long. Just think of it as a prevent defense."

She frowned and studied him with skepticism. "Prevent defense?"

Joe took her hand as if to plead his case. "Two prevents for the price of one. The coat is long enough to prevent those jocks from going ballistic when they see that dress. And by spending money on you, I was prevented from buying booze."

Annie laughed. "I don't believe that for one minute. That's just an excuse. Besides, the coat comes off when I get to the ballroom. I'd look a little odd wearing this coat on the dance floor, don't you think? So if you want to defend my honor, you'll have to take me to the dance, Joe. Being with me is the only real prevent defense you have."

"You're sure you want to do that?"

"Why wouldn't I?"

"I don't know. I just wondered. You seemed to have turned your back on the world. I can understand that."

"Yes, I think you can. Maybe we need to change that together."

"What if somebody recognizes you? Won't that be a problem for you? I mean, I wouldn't want to make you uncomfortable in front of the press, and I know they'll be out in full force."

He was concerned about her. That touched her. Could she do it? It had once been so easy. Could she become Annise again for one night? Just for a moment she felt a sense of unease sweep over her, then she shook it off. "You don't have to worry about that. I really don't look like I used to. This is a new face I'm wearing. There's only one person who'd stand a chance of recognizing the old me, and she hasn't tracked me down so far. If I run into her, well, we'll help each other. Deal?"

Joe couldn't stop himself from putting his finger beneath her chin and tilting her face up so that he could see it for himself. "I'm glad you don't look the same. There's something special about knowing this face doesn't belong to the world. It's like you're all new and shiny for me. Nobody has put smudges on you yet."

The smudges are there, Joe. They're just on the inside where they can't be seen.

There was something disturbingly intimate about sharing the bathroom to get ready—Annie rolling her hair in hot curlers while Joe used the mirror to shave. She hadn't been certain, until he started to get ready, whether Joe was going.

Once she decided that he was, she finished her hair and moved her things downstairs so that the ongoing tension between them would be defused. So much for that idea. It certainly wasn't working. He hadn't kissed her again, but she wanted him to. He touched her sparingly, but she felt his hands on her when they weren't even close.

She caught herself smiling as she heard him moving around overhead. A *thump, thump, thump* brought visions of his hopping on one foot while he put his leg into his trousers. A second set of thumps confirmed this theory. He was actually whistling again, though she didn't recognize the song.

Annie dressed quickly, pulling on the gold-flecked hose and high-heeled shoes and the short, elastic dress. In the half bath downstairs, she applied her makeup and combed her hair into a great mass of golden curls. She was adding a touch of spray to her hair when he came down the stairs, his attention on his wrists.

"You're going to have to help me here, Annie. I'm all thumbs."

She glanced up at him in his shiny black shoes, trousers, and pleated white shirt open to reveal his massive chest. No, he was wrong. He was all man, all golden and bright, his blond hair still damp and mussed, his shirtsleeves flopping as he tried to thread cuff links through the buttonholes.

"I can see you need help. Let me," she said, holding out her hand.

He pulled the stud out and lifted his head, ready to hand it to her, then froze. "Oh darling! They're back, the legs and that dress. A coat won't do it, I need a tent."

Annie laughed at Joe's stunned reaction. She didn't want to admit how good it felt to have him appreciate how she looked.

She couldn't resist teasing him. "You like the way I look?"

"Not fair, Annie, to an ineligible receiver."

"Time out, big guy." Annie let out a soft laugh and took the cuff links and button studs. "I thought you'd be an expert on dressing for a formal evening."

"No, ma'am. I'm an expert on undressing, and there's nothing formal about that. Why don't I just show you how simple it is? Is there a zipper to that body suit you're wearing?"

Now he was teasing her, and she couldn't resist responding with a smile. "Joe, be still or we'll never get there."

"Are you sure we have to go?"

"I'm sure, Joe. They're expecting us. Better hurry or we'll be late."

"Don't I get a reward for being still?" He didn't dare relax his tensed muscles or he'd never be able to keep his promise not to touch Annie.

She didn't dare look at him any longer from

such close range or she'd forget the promise she'd exacted. "Do you think you deserve one?"

"Probably not," was the best he could do. "I'm poison for you, Annie. I know it, but I just can't make myself recall a thing. Blackouts, remember?"

"There was a time I had blackouts. The therapist said it was self-imposed amnesia."

"Don't suppose you could manage one right now, a blackout spell, I mean. Then I could have one kiss to keep me going, and you could just forget that it happened."

She had leaned closer and closer with every exchange. Now their lips were only a breath apart. She didn't think she answered, but she must have. For only seconds later Joe was kissing her, hungrily, eagerly, possessively. Then, just as she felt his erection throbbing against her, she pushed him away.

"A kiss, Armstrong, that's all you get," she said, taking a deep breath.

"Annie, remind me to tell Rob to rent trousers with pleats the next time he takes it upon himself to choose a tux for me. When I'm around you, these pants constitute an illegal formation. Unless I want to get thrown out of the game, I'd better get off the field."

He didn't seem disturbed as he did an about-face and marched slowly up the stairs. Moments later, when he returned, he was wearing his jacket and his feisty red bow tie. His hair was combed to perfection.

"Shall we take the Jeep, Angel?" he said, crooking his arm in invitation. "Or had you rather fly?"

The evening was magical. As if by consent, both Annie and Joe put the past three days behind them, determined to be, just for this night, two people out on the town. A safari-costumed valet opened the door to the Jeep and visibly choked as he assisted Annie out.

Joe wagged his finger in the face of the stunned young man and whirled Annie around, threading his arm around her waist. "I think you've taken his breath away, darling."

"I think you're doing pretty well yourself," she said, nudging him into noticing the two women just inside the lobby who'd stopped in their tracks and were staring openly at Joe.

He marshaled them through the lobby and up the grand staircase to the atrium, where tables had been set around the dance floor and orchestra podium. Giant snowflakes and silver streamers glittered, balls of metallic light whirled, casting a myriad of color around the room. And everywhere sleekly elegant men and glamorous women called out greetings to Joe.

"Hey, man, get your butt over here and let me look at that creature you're with."

It was Ace, wearing a tux with a plaid vest and matching tie. His wife brightened at the sight of Annie and moved toward her.

"I'm so glad you came," she said. "I was afraid that I wouldn't know anyone here."

Ace stared at Annie curiously. "You know Lois?"

"Of course," Annie replied. "We met the night of your accident, remember? How are you, Lois?"

Ace furrowed his brow and squinted at her. "Yeah, I guess I do. By the time I left the hospital, things began to get pretty hazy. It must have been the lick on the head."

"Or the alcohol," his wife said. "Do sit with us so I won't feel like the outcast at the Sunday-school picnic."

Annie slipped her arm around the pregnant woman and allowed her to direct their steps to a table in the corner. "Why on earth would you say a thing like that?"

"It's all these women. They're so beautiful and so smart. I'm just a mountain girl from Kentucky."

"How's it hanging, dude?" Ace said, slapping Joe on the back.

Joe bit back a slang reply and said instead, "How're you doing? Did you get in trouble about the accident?"

"Yeah, don't I always? Coach fined me and gave me the usual crap about being history. I needed you to run interferences, Joe. Where were you?"

"Sorry, Ace, I've got enough on my own plate right now." Joe heard the bravado in Ace's voice, but he knew that his friend was hurting. He'd learned how to cover up his own fear with the same kind of cool jive talk. But Ace wasn't fooling him.

"Why don't you stop the drinking, old buddy? It doesn't help anything and you're only hurting Lois. She doesn't deserve this."

Ace cut his eyes toward Lois and back to Joe. "Hell, I know it, man. But I'm going crazy trying to hold on. If I get cut, then what do I do?"

"You live, Ace. You're not like me. You have a wife and a kid coming. So what if you're a step slower? Find a place with a slower track."

"When you coming back, man? We need you and that gimpy knee. I need you. That new kid throwing the ball may have the arm, but he don't have the smarts."

"I've lost it, Ace. But you haven't. Not yet. You've got a baby coming and a wife who loves you. Get your life together while you still can."

"You know what you sound like, Joe? A damn preacher, that's what. What do you know about it? For five years I averaged over a hundred yards a game and scored at least one touchdown. Ah, hell, let's get a drink."

Annie was half listening as the two men conversed. When Ace started toward the bar, she gave Joe a pointed nod. He resisted for a moment, then turned and followed Ace, turning back to give Annie a frown before being swallowed up by the crowd.

"So how long have you and Joe been together?" Lois asked.

"Three days," Annie said, and studied the people sitting at the tables in front of them.

"Only three days?" she argued in disbelief. "I don't believe that. He's practically touching you with those big ol' blue love eyes."

Annie laughed. "Love eyes? I'm not sure that's what I'd call them. Lust maybe. How long have you and Ace been together?"

"I been Ace's lady for nine years. But I wouldn't marry him until now."

Annie cut her eyes back toward Lois. "Why not?"

"I never thought he really wanted me. You know how athletes are; they chase after everything in skirts. I didn't want him to be unfaithful, and if we weren't married, he wouldn't be."

"Why'd you change your mind?"

"He needs me now and the baby needs him. I thought that would be enough. But maybe I was wrong."

"I hope not, Lois. Ace loves you, I'm sure. Why else would he have wanted to marry you?"

"'Cause he was scared, I think, and he don't want nobody to know. But I do. Just like your man, Joe. You going to marry him?"

"Heavens no. We're just friends."

Annie felt someone behind her before she heard a familiar voice. "Hello, Annie," Rob's voice cut in. "Glad to see you made it. Where's your date?"

"He and Ace went to the bar. Do you know Lois?"

At the shake of his head, Annie introduced them. "Will you join us, Rob?"

"Only if you'll dance with me first. I want to get a good look at the dress that Joe didn't want me to see." He held out his hand and pulled Annie toward the crowded floor.

The orchestra was playing an old Bing Crosby tune from the forties. Annie allowed Rob to pull her close and gave herself over to the music. He hummed and maneuvered her through the mass.

"I don't know where you came from, Annie, but I hope you're going to stay around for a while."

"Why?"

"You're good for Joe. I haven't seen him interested in anything or anybody in months. I know he got hurt, but the doctor says he's ready for some light playing time. His arm isn't as accurate as it once was, but he's still the smartest quarterback in the league."

Annie raised her chin, not certain of what she was hearing. "You mean he isn't washed up?"

"Hell, no. The only washing he's done is to himself. Sure, he's not the Falcons' number-one man now, but Jones is grooming him as an offensive assistant. At least he was until Joe got on this path to self-destruction."

"And when was that?"

"I don't know. Started at the end of the summer, just before the season started. He seemed to accept his new backup role and I thought he was adjusting to it. Then Jack died—and *whammo!*

Halfway into the schedule Joe got hurt and he was gone."

"I don't know why, but I thought he had retired."

"He thinks he has too. He hasn't even been to practice for the last month. But I'll have to give it to his coach, he hasn't given up and traded him."

"Would he be able to do that?"

"He could. But Jones made the transition from player to coach and he still believes that Joe can do it too."

The music came to an end and the band struck up another tune. Rob kept dancing. "I think he's a natural but I can't get through to him. I was hoping that you had."

"I don't know a thing about football. But he did say he was financially set for life."

Rob looked at her with a puzzled expression. "He is. Is that important to you?"

"Of course not. But it's important to him. If he's going to end his career without having financial stability, he's more likely to be a casualty. That would make my job harder."

"Job?" Rob frowned as he tried to make sense out of her line of thinking. He would have asked more, except Joe appeared at Annie's back and turned her around and into his arms.

"As my agent, Rob, you may get as much of my money as I do, but my girl isn't included in my salary. That means you get zilch." Joe was actually angry, staring at Rob with murder in his eyes at the same time as he wore a false smile on his lips for anyone who watched. "Why didn't you wait for me, darling?" he said as he turned toward her.

She was having trouble answering. The crowd of dancers pressed against them, pushing her even closer to the man who'd set his arms around her as if she were a treasure and he were the vault protecting it. "Why didn't you stay with me?"

"I should have. But that turkey Ace had to have a drink. I decided he'd be better off if I went with him instead of leaving him on his own. Poor Lois. I don't know what's wrong with Ace."

"I don't know what's wrong with you either," she said, considering what she'd learned and the reason she'd been sent to rescue Joe. "You're both men with problems."

He pulled her closer, then grinned at her. "Yeah! And we both got women who can take care of them."

"Yeah, and Ace's problem got Lois pregnant when she fell for his sweet talk."

"You don't want to have children, Annie?"

She couldn't tell whether he was serious or talking nonsense. "Of course I want—wanted to have children. But that's unlikely to happen now."

The heavy bulge of his arousal was unmistakable. Caught out in the midst of a crowd, there was little she could do about it, and she began to feel that old frisson of panic. Half of her was responding. The other half wanted to turn and run. It didn't help that Rob was suggesting that she could help Joe find himself.

It didn't help that Mac was suggesting that Joe could help Annie learn to face her past.

"Why would you think you can't have children?"

"Because the last man who rubbed his body against mine the way you're doing took away the possibility."

She jerked away from him and made her way across the dance floor toward Lois, whose eyes looked a bit watery. "I'm going to powder my nose," she said. "Wanna go?"

A look of relief swept across the woman's face. "Sure. Let me tell Ace." Moments later they were pressing through the new arrivals and into the powder room.

"I know why I'm in a hurry to get here," Lois joked, "but what's your excuse?"

"Let's just say that my date got penalized for an illegal formation."

Lois smiled. "I like you, Annie. And I wouldn't want to have to fight with Joe over you."

"What does that mean?"

"It means that if fury could throw a football, Ace's hand would be burning now. What did you say to Joe?"

"Simple, I just said time out."

"Maybe, but from the look on his face, I'd say he thinks he's being thrown out of the game."

"No. I couldn't do that, Lois. I don't want him

to lose. Of course, I don't want him to win either. Ah, hell, I don't know what I want."

Lois grinned. "Yes you do, girl, you want him. And according to Ace, you've got him so tied up in knots that he's just about ready to concede defeat. What would you say to having a maid of honor who looks like she swallowed a pumpkin?"

"I'd say your pumpkin will turn into a jack-o'-lantern before that ever happens. I'm not interested in Joe as a man, Lois. This is a business transaction."

Lois didn't even try to conceal her disbelief. "Sure it is. Bedroom business, maybe."

"It's true. I'm here on assignment."

Lois turned a shrewd eye on Annie. "Tell it to the IRS. That and a quarter will get you a phone call to your lawyer when you end up behind bars."

Lois excused herself and moved into the back room, leaving Annie sitting on one of the satin stools checking her makeup in the mirrors. She could hear the conversation of two women from around the corner where the lounge area was.

"Did you see Joe Armstrong?" the first one asked, practically drooling.

"Joe Armstrong, the Stud of the South," the second speaker said in a flippant manner. "He's the reason I'm here. His manager invited me, insisted that Joe wanted me to come. All those managers find a way to put the spotlight on their boys. Rob is better than most."

"I didn't know you and Joe were friends."

"We're not, Mary Ellen. Never even met the man. But I knew his manager, Rob, very well at one time."

"If Rob looks anything like Joe, I'd like to meet him."

The second speaker said something in a low voice, something that Annie couldn't hear, ending with, ". . . must be the woman he's with. Who is she?"

It was obvious that the drooler wasn't interested in Joe's companion. "Companion? Didn't know he was with anybody. What did she look like?"

"Like she stepped straight off the cover of *Cosmo* and landed in the center of *Playboy*. I tell you, Mary Ellen, there's something vaguely familiar about her. I've seen her somewhere before."

Kiki? Annie felt her heart stop. Of all the people in the world to face, Kiki Mitchell was probably her worst nightmare. And Rob had invited her.

"You're just jealous, Kiki. You think every woman you meet is some refugee from your award-winning past. You've got a nose for news, all right. When you're hot, you're hot. But nobody's hot all the time."

"Maybe," the woman called Kiki said. "And when you're not, you're not. But there've been damned few times in my life when I was wrong on a hunch. Why else do you think I'm down here in this redneck town covering a celebrity ball?"

"Same reason I'm here. Because Kevin Costner

is making a picture in Atlanta, and he's going to make an appearance, that's why. He's prime-time news."

"Sure, and don't we wish we were."

"I don't know. Working for *StarWatch* pays your bills, Ms. Mitchell, and gives you access to all the beautiful people. You wouldn't change places with a regular newspaper photographer for all the tea in China, and neither would I."

"No, Mary Ellen, it's more than that. My life has been a series of being-in-the-right-place-at-the-right-time photos. Even I don't know how in hell it happens."

Annie sat frozen in her seat. The tabloid photographer Kiki Mitchell had made Annise her life's work, shooting hundreds of photographs over the years. She'd even slipped into the hospital the night Annie was supposed to have died, taking the only photograph that ever made the tabloids, the stark shot of a face mutilated and a woman destroyed.

Annie only found that out later, at the same time she learned that her stalker had turned his knife inward, stabbing himself in the heart.

Now Kiki was here, at the Winter Ball, the first public appearance of Annie Calloway. And Rob had invited her. For what? *Hold on, Annie, don't be paranoid. He had no way of knowing about you and what it would mean to have Kiki here.* It shouldn't have mattered, but Annie couldn't help but believe that fate had stepped in and taken over.

Annie Calloway's life was flashing before her eyes. Annise had come back from the dead on the arm of Joe Armstrong, the one athlete in the world who always drew every camera in the house.

And Kiki Mitchell was ready to record it.

NINE

"Ready, Annie?"

Lois was standing behind her, looking at her in the powder-room mirror. "Hey, girl? You're as white as a sheet. Are you okay?"

Annie didn't know whether she answered or not. But she did stand and follow Lois toward the door, all the while letting her mind replay the conversation she'd just heard. Kiki Mitchell was in the same city, in the same hotel, with her camera.

How could it have happened? What were the odds that it could happen? It had to be coincidence. As an agent, Rob was responsible for getting his client good press. Kiki Mitchell was in town covering Kevin Costner's appearance at the ball. Why wouldn't Rob alert Kiki to Joe's presence? He had no way of knowing what that would mean to Annie. What should she do?

The trek back to their table would carry them

along the shadows around the back of the atrium toward the orchestra. Shadows were safe, but the location of the table put them deeper into the room and away from the door. She could be caught back there in a place from which she couldn't escape. Annie stopped, hesitating as she considered her options.

"Are you sure you're all right, girlfriend?" Lois was saying in her ear.

"Yes, I'm fine. Really, I'm fine," Annie reassured the pregnant woman. "You go back to the men. I think I need some air." She whirled around and started toward the escalator leading to the lower ballroom area.

Kiki was right. There was no reason, no odds big enough to explain fate taking a hand. Joe wouldn't have told Rob about her. She knew Joe well enough to trust him with her secret.

At that moment the movie star and his entourage appeared at the head of the moving staircase. Before Annie could move out of their path, a series of flashes temporarily blinded her, causing her to pause.

Seconds later a woman brushed past her to get a better shot.

"Excuse me," the photographer said, giving Annie no more than a cursory glance. Then she stopped and turned back with a curious expression on her face. "Say, do I know you?" she began.

"Annie!" Joe's voice called out, reaching her

side just as the mass of people lurched forward toward Kevin Costner, pushing her out of the way.

Freed from the onlookers, Annie found the top step of the escalator and started down, followed by Joe, who didn't understand what was happening. "Annie, what's wrong?"

She strode across the marbled floor, reached the elevators, and ducked around the potted trees strung with twinkling lights. As she moved she knew she was being watched and her actions weren't helping her cause. Forcing herself, she stopped and turned toward Joe, glancing over his shoulder at the woman studying her from the balcony above, the woman whose camera had focused on Annise so many times, the woman who was now taking a picture of her with Joe.

"Dammit, Annie! I said stop!" Joe reached out and took hold of her arm, turning her around. "What's wrong, did one of those turkeys make a pass at you?"

She managed to shake her head as she buried it into his shoulder, whispering a muffled, "No."

"Then what is it?"

"I thought I could do it, Joe. Come to something like this. I thought I was past all that. But the people, the hype. I didn't expect—I mean I thought no one would know. Why did he do it, Joe?"

"Do what? Who knows what?"

"Rob brought a photographer here."

"Rob's passion in life is getting me press,

whether I want it or not. Why does that bother you?"

"Coming here may have ruined everything."

"I don't have any idea what you're talking about, Annie. Let's get out of here," he finally said, sheltering her with his arm as they headed for the exit. "I never wanted to come in the first place."

"My coat," she said. "My coat is upstairs."

"To hell with the coat. I'll buy you another one." He took off his jacket and draped it around her shoulders, handing his ticket to the valet at the door. "Get the Jeep here, quick!"

Almost before she knew what had happened, they were in Joe's Jeep, pulling out of the hotel parking area and heading north.

They drove for a while, Joe not asking questions, Annie not forming answers to those that would come. She felt like a fool. She'd been so full of herself. So certain that all her fears were behind her. Joe needed help. She'd provided it. She'd survived. She had all the answers. But she didn't. One glance by a photographer who couldn't possibly have known who she was, and she'd shriveled up and died. No, she hadn't died. She wouldn't do that. She was angry, not upset. She was in charge of her fate and she had no intention of backing down.

"I thought you wanted to go with Ace," he finally said, "or I never would have gone."

"I did. I just didn't expect that would happen."

He kept his voice calm. "What would happen, darling?"

"The photographer. Didn't you see her? She was looking right at you, at me, taking our picture. She recognized me. I know she did."

"Aren't you being a little paranoid? You said that you don't look at all like you did before. What makes you think she knew who you were?"

"Because she was standing right by Kevin Costner and she was taking a picture of me. No photographer would do that, unless," she asked, suddenly hopeful, "is Kiki Mitchell a fan of yours?"

"Sorry, Annie. I don't think so."

"Then I was right. She recognized me. There is no other answer."

"You're wrong, darling. There's a simple explanation for her taking your picture instead of Costner's," Joe said.

"Oh? What?"

"Any photographer in his right mind would know where the real picture is. It's the legs, Annie, love. The legs."

"But this photographer was a woman."

"Doesn't matter, it had to be the legs. Have you ever seen Costner's legs? No comparison, darling. And he certainly couldn't walk in those heels."

Suddenly the absurdity of his reply broke over her and she began to laugh. That laughter broke the tension, and Annie realized how irrationally she'd behaved.

"Oh, Joe, I'm sorry. You're right. I'm being paranoid. I actually thought that she knew who I was. I even thought for a moment that you'd set it up. I ruined everything. I dragged you away from the party before you even got involved. That's just what I'm not supposed to do. What is Mac going to say?"

"Who the hell cares what Mac says. I'm beginning to get a little tired of the mysterious Mac. He seems to know so much about me, about what I need. If he's so all-powerful, why is he so absent?"

"That's the way he works, Joe. Nobody ever gets to know Mac, not face-to-face."

"Then how come you are so well acquainted with him?"

"Because I couldn't see him. My face was bandaged. I never got a good look at him. Nobody ever has. Then, later, he used the phone."

"Whee! This is beginning to sound more and more like *The Twilight Zone*. This person, this Mac, rescued you and sent you someplace to recover. Then he recruited you to save me from disaster. Then what? I go out and save somebody else?"

"Probably. In fact I think you already have your assignment, Joe."

He didn't like what he was thinking. He didn't like it that what she was saying was beginning to make some kind of sense. "Ace?"

"Of course I can't be sure," Annie said. "But maybe. Of course you'll have to want to do it. Mac never forces anybody."

Joe left the highway and turned into the two-lane road that led to his house. The streetlights and automobiles were left behind, plunging them into thick black night. He let her answers circle around in his mind while he drove into the garage and parked the Jeep.

Then he sat for a moment in the darkness. "So now I not only have your salvation on my conscience, but I'm responsible for Ace and Lois and a baby? What do I get out of it?"

"You get your life back, or at least one that you can tolerate."

"What about you?"

"Me? Well, I'm not sure. I suppose Mac will give me a new assignment."

"What about what you want? When do you take charge of your life again, stop repaying your debt?"

"I can't answer that, Joe. I've only now reached the point where I could begin to believe that it was possible to take charge of my life. Until now, I thought I'd lost it all."

"Well, you haven't. And if that photographer back there did recognize you, you're going to have to decide whether you're Annise or Annie. No, I think you've got to do more than that. You don't even know who Annie is, do you?"

"Of course I do. I'm Annabelle Calloway. I'm—"

But she couldn't complete the sentence. Annabelle Calloway had become Annise and Annise had died. She was no longer either one. Annie was a shadow figure, created in a mountaintop rehabilitation center reserved for people who'd been reborn.

Joe waited in the darkness. When she didn't answer he jerked the door open and went inside, leaving her sitting there in the dark. Woodenly, Annie crawled out of the Jeep and followed him. Everything seemed to be collapsing around her.

Joe obviously had no intention of becoming Ace's retriever. As far as she could tell he was more concerned about her leaving than he was about rejoining the team. As for her past and the return of Kiki Mitchell in her life, she didn't even want to consider the potential for trouble that scenario held.

She'd have to tell Mac. Then she'd have to do what she should have done in the beginning—leave —before she destroyed any more people. While she still had some dignity left.

But she was avoiding the main issue. Who was Annie? And what would she be for the rest of her life? And what part did Joe play in it?

"Why are you whispering?" Mac asked.

"Because Joe is upstairs and I don't want him to know I'm calling you."

"Why?"

"He's feeling pressure. I think he's about to send me packing. Or maybe I'd just better leave. This wasn't working out, and now that woman is here, in Atlanta, taking my picture."

"What woman?"

"Kiki Mitchell, the photographer who took that

awful picture of me in the hospital, the one who showed the world what that maniac did to me."

Mac let out a deep sigh. "Well, we knew that would happen someday, Annie. Why are you so upset? You can handle one pesky photographer, can't you?"

"But Rob, Joe's agent, invited her."

"So, he probably invited everybody in the business. It's his job to see that Joe gets coverage. God knows he's been out of the spotlight for a while."

"But she knows who I am. She took my picture with Joe."

"So, she took your picture with Joe," Mac was saying. "What makes you think she had any idea who you were?"

"There was just something about the way she was looking at me."

"Annie Calloway, I've seen you in one of those skintight short dresses, and I've seen Joe Armstrong. Any photographer with one eye and half his wits would shoot your picture. What I'm more concerned about is Joe."

"Oh, Mac, I'm a failure. I'm no nearer to finding a way to give him a future than I was when I came."

"Really?" Mac was skeptical and he didn't bother to conceal it. "Before you arrived he'd avoided the team, avoided the telephone, and as far as I can tell, the only people he'd dealt with were the liquor-store owner and a couple of fast-food deliverymen. How many of those has he called since you came?"

"Well, none."

"And how much drinking has he done?"

"None."

"And where has he been?"

"Well, we went grocery shopping. We went to the hospital to get Ace. And we went to the ball."

"Not to speak of a personal shopping tour he went on, to have a coat altered to fit you," he added with his usual flair for the dramatic.

Annie wished she could have seen through her bandages. Mac was such an enigma, a master at theatrics. If he weren't a stage actor, he should have been.

"Oh, Mac, I'm confused. It isn't only Kiki Mitchell, it's me. It's Joe. It's what I'm beginning to feel. What am I going to do?"

"I've told you before, Annie, you'll know. When the time comes, you'll know."

Annie heard Joe's footsteps overhead. He was pacing back and forth in obvious agitation. She was still trying to figure out how things had gone so wrong when she heard the creak of the door hinge. He was coming down the stairs.

"Gotta go, Mac. I hear Prince Charming headed my way."

"Annie?" Joe called out. "Where are you?"

Annie hung up the phone and turned to face Joe as he came into the kitchen. The room suddenly got smaller with his presence.

"I think we ought to talk."

Annie took a deep breath, trying to hold on to her composure. Her conversation with Mac had rattled her more than she'd believed possible. Everything seemed to be changing. All her newly found peace and beauty were collapsing in the wake of her own uncertainties.

This is a scene you're playing, Annie. Approach it that way. Both of you are confused and angry. He thinks he wants you to go. The truth is, you want to go. But you can't. You don't understand what is happening, but if you leave before you've accomplished your goal, you'll forever be a failure.

"I agree. I'm making coffee. Will you join me?"

She held out her hand as if she were saying, "Good morning, it's nice to meet you." He started to take it, then brushed past. He knew there was no way in hell that he could take her hand without sweeping her into his arms. As he moved past her he could see that she knew she'd been rejected. He couldn't let that sway him.

"Yes."

The terseness of his reply set the stage for Annie. He'd shed his suspenders and the studs in his shirt leaving it open, the crisply pleated white fabric making a kind of frame for his tantalizing chest. Her gaze was drawn there, to the dark golden hair that made a V across his muscular body. As happened the moment before she stepped in front of the camera, all the air whooshed out of her lungs, leaving her light-headed and unsteady.

Ah, Annie, where's your control? To cover her shaking hands she turned to the sink, filling the coffeepot with water and measuring two scoops of ground beans. Reaching across the wide counter, she plugged the pot into the wall.

For a man who wanted to talk, Joe seemed to be having as much trouble as she. *You'll know when the time comes.* That's what Mac had said. But she didn't. The coffee began to flow through the filter. She watched it, not seeing it but unable to turn around.

"I'm sorry, Joe," she said finally. "I've handled everything badly. It's just that suddenly I don't know who I am."

There was a silence. "What do you mean, who you are?"

"I mean I was a little nobody when I was Annabelle Calloway. Then I got lucky and landed those modeling jobs. Once I became Annise, I was somebody. But Annise died."

"So, you're Annie now. Is that a problem?"

She thought for a moment. "No, it's just that I'm not sure who Annie is."

"Who do you want her to be?"

"I thought she was a person who could give, who could help people find peace. I wanted to help somebody else. I needed not to think about me anymore."

"And that's changing, isn't it?" Joe asked, adding gently, "It's hard, isn't it? You think you've got everything under control, and suddenly you learn that nothing is what you thought. You're changing, Annie, and maybe that's all right."

"I don't think I like this part of my job."

"Am I hearing regret, Annie?"

Pain caught her by surprise. Pain and uncertainty. She couldn't tell Joe because she didn't understand it all yet. "Sure," she said flippantly. "I regret losing my coat," she admitted with more than a little catch in her throat.

Joe saw the tension in her backbone and futility in her bowed head. "I don't think it's just the coat. Does Cinderella regret leaving the ball?"

"No!" she snapped. "Only that I left my beautiful coat."

Only that I may be discovered before I'm ready for the world to know. Before I've made you understand about tomorrow and a future.

"Well, it isn't a glass slipper, Annie, but, hey, these are the nineties. Nobody, but nobody, wears glass anymore." Joe swore and slapped the table. "I'm sorry, Annie. Now I'm being a smart-ass, and you're hurting. We're both hurting."

"What's wrong, Joe?" She turned and hurried to where he was sitting.

"What's wrong?" He looked up at her, caught the expression of concern in her eyes, and lost every attempt at restraint he could have made. He couldn't even carry on a conversation with the woman. His throat ached. His groin was twisted so tight that he felt like a corkscrew. "You're messing up my mind, that's what's wrong."

"What have I done now?"

"You're driving me crazy, Annie, that's what's wrong. I can't keep my hands off you any longer."

"I'm sorry. I never intended to make it hard for you."

He couldn't hold back a chortle as he planted his chin against his chest, closed his eyes, and gritted his teeth.

"Oh, Joe. All I wanted to do was help." She moved against him, pulling his head to her breast, just holding him for a long moment before whispering, "I'm so sorry. This isn't working out, is it?"

With another groan he spread his legs, drawing her closer, adjusting his body so that she fit snugly between his thighs. "Damned if I know. You've turned me inside out, Annie. If you wanted to make me feel something besides guilt, you've done it. But now I'm hurting you. That's not fair."

"I'm not sure being fair matters," she whispered, fighting the heat that had swept over her. His touch was instant meltdown, liquefying even her bones. "I don't understand what is happening. I just want you. . . ."

"I want you, too, Annie. I want you so much I can't see straight. I want to slide my fingertips up your leg and see what my touch does to your bare skin. I want to be inside you, making you cry out with need. I want you to need me the way I need you."

As he spoke his fingers moved slowly along the

outside of her thigh, inching their way up Annie's body, setting off a firestorm of sensation.

"Oh, Joe," she protested, her voice barely a whimper. "I don't know. Don't you understand? I don't know if I can be with you—no matter how much I want to."

"Yes you can, Annie. You see, Mac was wrong. When Annise died, a part of you died as well. You can't become some new person without healing the old."

"But I don't want to be Annise anymore. You're right about me. I like Annie. Or I think I will if she ever learns who she is."

"Sure you like her. Annie wears a mask. She isn't real. She's some character you're playing on a stage. Mac is the playwright, and you're his creation."

"And what are you, Joe? You're hiding out here, avoiding everybody you were ever close to. What does that make you?"

"I don't know. But at least the only person I'm hurting is me."

"Not anymore, Joe. You're hurting me." Annie said, feeling a great well of emotion tear through her. Moisture crept into her eyes, and she felt herself tremble inside Joe's arms.

Joe tightened his grip on her waist. "No! I stopped letting myself feel need. That's the only way I can be certain that I won't hurt anybody."

She took a deep breath and told Joe the truth. "You're too late, Joe. *I* need you. You're the only one I've even let touch me since—since that night. This is the closest I've been to a man without having a panic attack. I need you, Joe Armstrong, and I don't want to change that."

He raised his head and looked up at her closed eyes, her pale face, her anguish. She'd asked him to make love to her before. She'd told him that she was no longer a real, feeling woman, but he hadn't believed her. He'd thought she was just using herself to force him to go along with whatever game she'd been playing.

Annie had come to help him, sent there by this Mac to pull him back from the deep depression he'd fallen into. And she'd done it. He'd stopped thinking about his past and started to worry about hers. No, he'd started to think about their present. He'd even stopped at the pet shop and bought a large sack of food for the geese and some birdseed.

"I won't be good for you, Annie. Find yourself a man without the emotional baggage I carry around."

She might have been alarmed if she hadn't felt how gently he was holding her. "I don't want to find another man, Joe. If we can't get rid of that baggage, I'll help you carry it."

"You're not strong enough to do that. I saw how fragile you were when you were holding on to me at the hotel."

"That was different. That was about me. I may not be on real steady ground with my past yet, but I know what I want."

"And what's that?"

Gaining courage with every beat of her racing heart, she tightened her muscles and kissed him.

She closed her lips over his, determined to let her feelings run free, to give as much as she got. This time there was no pillow between them, no holding back, no reticence.

And then she wasn't forcing herself anymore. Her fingernails were digging into Joe's back, lifting, pulling him up so that they were pressed against each other. Nothing had ever felt so right before. Wrenching away from him, she leaned back and looked up at him.

"Don't hurt me, Joe," she whispered.

"I'd never hurt you," he promised, his voice so low and tight that she could barely understand. "But you'll have to tell me, let me know if I move too fast."

"I'll try."

He kissed her, gently, softly, probing her mouth as if he'd never kissed a woman before. "You're so sweet, so soft." With one hand he held her chin and continued to plant light little kisses across her neck, her eyelids, her nose. With the other hand he'd started drawing little circles around her shoulder, catching the stretchy fabric of her dress and moving it down her upper arms.

"I like women who sound as if they're breathless. Do I take your breath away, Annie?"

"Yes."

Her breath and her strength. Her legs had

turned to foreign bodies that didn't seem to know their purpose. Before his lips reached the indention at the base of her neck, she was clasping her arms around his, trying to stand.

"Do you know how beautiful you are, Annie? How much I want you? From that first night when I opened the door and saw you standing there in the doorway like some angel, I knew."

"You did?"

"Don't talk, Annie. Just listen and feel. He was touching her breast now. Somehow her dress had slid down her body and he was holding her, caressing her nipple with his fingertip, then his tongue. "Does that make you writhe? Are you trembling, Annie?"

"My knees," she managed to say. "They won't hold me up."

"I'll hold you up. I'll carry you. Kiss me, Annie, as I pick you up. Kiss me again the way you did before."

She could hardly breathe as he leaned down and slipped his arm beneath her knees, lifting her effortlessly. His shirt was off his shoulders, and her breasts were grazing his bare chest, rasping back and forth as he started toward the stairs.

When they were in the bedroom, he let her down, peeling her dress down her body as her feet reached the floor.

"Christ!" he swore. "I'm looking at you and I don't believe it."

As if she were in a daze she opened her eyes and

became instantly impaled by the heat of his gaze. He was looking at her body. For a moment she wanted to close her eyes, turn away, and slam the door to the room behind her. Then she forced herself to see what he was seeing. The dress was gone, leaving only the thigh-high lace gold stockings with the little band of black velvet at the upper edge, and the wisp of gold lacy underwear that barely covered the golden hair beneath.

She reached down to remove the gold strappy shoes.

"No, don't. Leave them on. Leave it all on. Just stand there and let me look at you while I get out of these clothes."

She couldn't have moved if she'd wanted. Joe unfastened the hook on his black trousers and let them fall to the floor, exposing black briefs that were just as revealing. He pushed off his shiny black shoes, leaving only the black-ribbed socks.

"Oh, Joe." She took a step toward him. "You're —you've got the right name."

"What's that, the all-American boy?"

What she was seeing was no boy. What she was seeing was a man, exciting beyond belief. "No. I was referring to Stud of the South."

He grinned.

She groaned. "I'm sorry. That was crude of me. I'm not usually like that. I think it's the stockings and the high heels. I feel like a model on a pinup calendar."

He inched forward, until they were almost

touching. He could feel the heat coming from her. "You've got what every man in the world wants every month. That look would melt an iceberg."

"That's what my directors used to say. Give us 'the look,' Annise."

"What's the look?"

She lowered her chin and tilted her head saucily, half closed her eyes until she felt as if she were peeking out from under her lids, and parted her lips, licking them slowly as she whispered, "This is the look. It's an invitation to pleasure. Will you accept?"

"Oh, lady. I'm yours. Whatever you want, you've got it."

Suddenly all the strength seemed to drain out of her, and she collapsed on the edge of the bed. "Of course you will. Men always did. That was Annise's trademark, the bedroom look. You didn't have a chance. But it isn't real, Joe. That was Annise, not Annie."

Joe came to stand in front of her. "Annie, darling, give me your hand."

She did. He pulled her up and kissed her lightly. Then moved her hand down between them, pressing it against his arousal. "Annie, this is what *you* do to me, not the look, not some sex-kitten pose. I've gone around in misery since I first laid eyes on you and you weren't doing anything to cause it."

"You have?"

"I'd want you even if I were impotent, God forbid. But it wouldn't matter. I'd—we'd find a way to be together. Now I'm going to put you on this bed and lie down beside you. I'll take off your shoes because I don't want them to become lethal weapons, but where we go from there is up to you. Just don't give me any more invitations or I'll be tossed out of the game, and this is one time I don't want to be sent to the showers early."

Annie blushed as she realized that her hand was beneath his briefs and she was tugging on him and rubbing him against her. "Oh, I'm sorry."

"No you're not, you're enjoying every minute of torturing me."

He lifted her, feasted for a moment on her breast, then placed her reverently on the bed, lying beside her, his elbow bent, his head resting on one hand.

The light in the hallway spilled into the room, casting a golden glow across the floor, but not reaching the bed. There was no sound, no music, no conversation. Only the two of them and the growing intensity of their desire.

"I'm going to make love to you, Annie Calloway. I'm going to show you who Annie really is. You're going to know when the sun comes up that this Annie and Joe will never be the same again. They'll be a part of each other."

TEN

Joe took her hand and kissed her fingertips. She didn't pull away, but he could feel her uncertainty. Hers was no greater than his. This was all new for him, this kind of loving. But it was something he had to do. Making things right for Annie would be a kind of redemption.

Now you need a choir behind you, he thought. If this were a movie, the music would pick up its volume and the viewers would know that a crisis moment had arrived.

Crisis? Hell, if they played a tape of his pulse rate, they wouldn't need any other soundtrack. He made an effort to control his emotion. There was an ache inside him, a yearning that had to be held back, restrained.

Loving Annie was more than a pleasure; it was a giving of something he'd never expected to give. And if he never did another right thing in his life, this had to be right—for her. He moved from her fingers to her lips, softly, tentatively.

When she began to kiss him back, he pulled away. "Slowly, darling. We have all night." He pushed her hair behind her ear, kissing her lobe, rimming it with his tongue. On purpose he avoided touching her with his body. "You're so beautiful, Annie."

Just for a second she flinched, and he knew that being called beautiful bothered her. He was an idiot. Of course it did. That's what everybody else in the world had always told her. Her beauty had led that crazy man to stalk her.

"Not only outside," he whispered doggedly, "but inside as well. Believe me, Annie, it's true."

"I'm not, Joe. I'm dishonest and that's not pretty. I lied to you about why I came, and I've let the world think I'm dead."

"You *were* dishonest, Annie. Just like me. But you didn't know it until now."

She reached across her body and ran her fingers through his hair, then down the cord in his neck. "I feel your pulse, Joe. It's flying."

"I know. If you weren't here in this bed, I'd probably go straight out the window."

She laughed lightly. "I thought I was the angel."

"You are. I'm a goose."

He kissed her again, this time letting his fingertips range across her shoulder and down to her rib cage, slowly, without emotion. As she relaxed under his gentle touch he let his kiss deepen and was rewarded with a move that brought her breast beneath his hand.

He shivered and pushed his tongue into her mouth, then withdrew it, nuzzling the corners of her lips. "I like your breasts. They're just the right size for my hand."

"You mean they're too small. I know. For a model they're considered perfect, but as a woman . . . well, you don't have to pretend to like them, Joe, I know I'm not big enough."

"I don't know . . . to a washed-up football player, they're pretty special." He moved away from her face and captured her nipple with his lips.

"You aren't washed up, Joe, you're just drawing up a new game plan."

"Yeah," he growled wickedly, "and this one is a whole lot more fun."

Annie tried to argue, to say she wasn't talking about what they were doing, but she couldn't seem to focus on anything but the fire he'd set inside her. Every one of her senses was enhanced, heightened beneath his touch.

"Joe . . ." she whispered, no longer concealing the urgency she was feeling.

He held her still, tenderly but firmly. "Not yet, Annie. Let me love you. I want to touch every part of you, make you know me, and let me learn your body." Her cheeks flamed, and she twisted away, trying to hide her embarrassment. "No, don't do that. I love the way your eyes light up, the way your mouth wrinkles, the little mewing sounds you make. Don't hold back, Annie. Open yourself up to those feelings. Tell me what you like."

"I wish I could. But I don't know what to say," she admitted miserably. "This isn't like one of the love scenes on my television show. This is real."

"Then don't try to talk. Let me do all the talking."

"But I want you to know that I've thought about this—about us—a lot."

He laughed softly. "I thought you might have."

She would have said more, but when he moved his hands down her body she could hardly breathe. He moved closer. She could feel his body against her. He was trembling, from holding back, from trying not to frighten her. That made the moment even more special. Joe didn't need to worry about her fear, not anymore. Any anxiety she might have felt was burning away in the heat of her desire.

"I love the way you make me feel, the way my skin reacts to your touch," he said. And then he kissed her again, with surprising gentleness in the midst of his need.

His fingers ranged across her stomach and moved lower until they found the apex of her legs and began to play across the wispy patch of hair shielding the source of her heat. His touch sent her pulse soaring even higher. She turned her head into his shoulder, inhaling the sweet scent of his body. He let his palm slip across her thigh, moving slowly up and down almost in a caress as his fingers parted her legs and duplicated the motion in the valley between.

Joe knew that she was ready for him. He was almost mad with wanting her and yet he was afraid. She'd been so badly scarred once. The mysterious Mac couldn't know, but this would be Joe's most important assignment as a retriever. He couldn't fail. Loving Annie was a gift he didn't deserve, and he felt his heart fill with joy.

She reached out for him, her eyes wide, her hands shaking. "Please, Joe?"

He couldn't contain himself any longer. Supporting himself on his arms, he moved over her, slowly, ready at any moment to pull back if he saw any sign of panic in her eyes.

There was none.

And there was no turning back. He almost went too far before he remembered, before reason took over, and at the risk of ruining the mood, he raised up and reached inside the drawer beside his bed.

Annie's eyes widened as she watched him.

"You're a spectacular man, Joe Armstrong."

"Close your eyes, Annie, and feel. Don't be afraid."

"Afraid? Oh, Joe. I'm not afraid. I'm dying of need." But it was more than need she felt. It was the warm, beautiful, loving knowledge that Joe cared about her. As aroused as he was, he hadn't taken advantage of her. He'd thought of her future, of what this might mean. From the first, in his own way, he'd protected her. And he still was.

When he lowered himself over her, she lifted herself to meet him, taking him deep inside as if she'd been waiting for him. He tried to pace himself. He didn't want to frighten her by smothering her with his body weight, but she soon reached up and pulled him down to her. And as the raging fire spiraled out of control, there was no mistaking the moment when her body exploded with sensation. His low shuddering moan fed the aftershocks of her release until at last he collapsed against her.

"Oh, Annie," he whispered, then lifted his head and peered at her anxiously. "Annie?"

She smiled and studied his beautiful face. "I'm fine, Joe. I've never been so fine."

"Let me move. I'm too heavy for you," he said, and began to move away.

"Not so fast, Bucko," she whispered impishly, "not without me." And as he turned she moved with him so that now she was on top and he had the goofy grin on his face.

He caressed her bottom, adjusting her so that she fitted just where she should over his body. "I really ought not bring this up, considering that I'm in uncharted territory here, but you know a condom isn't reusable."

"Don't you have more?"

"Am I going to need more?"

"Without a doubt."

"Are you sure?"

She was.

He nodded.
They did.

Day five started in a totally different way. Annie couldn't say that she'd made any headway in redirecting Joe's future, but at least she knew that, for now, he was happy.

"Twigs and raisins?" he asked with a twinkle in his eye.

"And orange juice and vitamins."

"What happened to the ginseng? Now is the time to cook it or brew it or whatever you do with it," he said as he dived into the cereal with exaggerated relish.

She felt a blush heat her cheeks. "Ginseng?"

"Sure, for stamina, both sexual and otherwise, isn't it? Looks like you knew what you were doing when we shopped."

"I didn't actually buy any," she admitted, suddenly busying herself at the stove. "I was just—joking."

"Ah, well then, I'll take a few extra vitamins. I'm sure I'll hold up."

Annie bit back a smile. Judging from his stamina the night before, the degree of his "holding up" was never in doubt. "About my assignment, Joe," she began. "Could we talk? I'm afraid that we got a bit off the track."

"I think we got on track, Annie. Before that we were just shadowboxing. You were looking for something for me to sink my teeth into. Well, we found it."

She was afraid to ask, but she blurted it out anyway. "What?"

Joe stood up and walked over to the stove, where he slipped his arms around her, holding her just beneath her breasts while he planted his chin on her shoulder. "Annie, call your buddy Mac and tell him that I'm going to need long-term care. Tell him you've found your subject. He's been redeemed and you're resigning."

Annie stiffened.

"What's wrong, darling?" Joe asked, confused by her reaction. "Surely you don't think that I'm going to give you up now that I've saved you? That's the first requirement of being a retriever—save and protect."

She managed to turn around and push him back. "Joe, you don't understand. It isn't me that we're saving, it's you. Now that you're . . . better, we have to get your future in gear."

"Future? You are my future, the only future I want."

"You don't understand. You have to change," she whispered, "for me to repay my debt.

"Annie, I *have* changed. There is no separate me and you anymore. I may not know what this is all about, but I know that this is *us*. And that's all the future I need."

So caught up in the wonder of her own feelings, she hadn't thought that far ahead. Could he be right? Was it possible that they were meant to be together? No, Mac had explained over and over that redemption had to come from the individual. It couldn't depend on anyone else. She couldn't use herself as the means by which Joe was turned around. Neither could she use him for her own purposes.

But she had. She'd done the very thing Mac had forbidden her to do. She'd fallen in love with her client. She'd spent a night in his arms . . . and . . . she wanted more. That changed everything.

Joe stepped back. He looked at her with disbelief on his face. "I don't believe you, Annie Calloway. You're a coward. You use all that wonderful motivational talk on me, and you're ready to run away when my future and yours overlap."

He was talking about overlapping futures, about their being together. He'd transferred his indecision to her. His future was dependent on her now. One set of problems had simply changed into another. She'd been warned about that; Mac had told her over and over. She just hadn't listened.

"No . . . I'm not running away. I mean I'm not sure. Oh, Joe. This wasn't supposed to happen. You can't depend on me."

"It's been a long time since I've been around two people who were committed to each other, Annie, but if I remember how it went, my folks depended on each other. And that didn't make either one of them weak."

He was so much more logical than she was. He didn't have to find any answers for next year. All he was concerned about was the now. He hadn't a clue about how long it had taken her to reach this point and how determined she was to succeed. She'd thought she was ready to face the world again, only she wasn't.

The fund-raiser had made all that too clear to her. She might have recovered physically and she might have thought she was ready to show her gratitude by helping others, but her own future was still a big question mark.

Mac might believe in her, but she couldn't hide from the truth any longer.

"I need to talk with Mac, Joe."

"To hell with Mac. This is between us, Annie. We don't need anybody to decide what we're doing."

"You don't understand, Joe. Nothing is resolved. So, we slept together. You proved to me that I can be with a man again. For that I'll always be grateful. But what about tomorrow? Where do we go from here?"

"Who knows? We don't have to decide everything at once. We take it one step at the time, starting with us."

Annie walked toward the window, looking out at the bright January sunshine. "No, Joe. There can't be an us until we deal with the past."

Joe clenched his hands in anger. He was about

to lose her, and he didn't seem to be able to stop it from happening. "So what are you going to do?"

"If you won't face your situation, I can't force you. But I can deal with mine. I'm going to see Kiki Mitchell."

"I'll go with you," he said quickly.

"No, I'll have to do this myself."

He was afraid to ask if she'd be back. And she didn't say.

Half an hour later a car came for Annie. She heard the horn and started toward the door, pausing only to say, "If you can't deal with your career as a ballplayer, at least deal with Jack's death." Then she was gone.

For the rest of the day he paced back and forth. It was clear that she wasn't going to help him face his demons. She'd done something more important. She'd made him understand that he had to do it alone.

The six o'clock news broke the story of the return of soap-opera star Annise. The details of her attack and years of hospitalization and recovery read like a horror story. Every channel and all the editorial shows were full of her miraculous recovery and the new face that was even more beautiful than the old one.

"What are your plans, Annise?" the reporter was asking.

Joe's heart ached as he watched the beautiful woman plant a confident expression on her face and answer their questions. "I have no plans yet, other than to spend some time considering my options."

"Will you go back to *Beyond Love*?"

"No, the show has gone on without me. Whatever I do will be new and rewarding."

She'd been answering questions steadily when one particular photographer stepped forward and snapped a picture. Then, lowering her camera, she said, "What about Joe Armstrong? Is he a part of your reward?"

After a silence she said softly, "I hope so. But I can't be sure."

"What about his career with the Falcons? According to management, he is still injured. But gossip is that he's left the team and won't play anymore this season. What happened?"

"I can only say that Joe has been suffering from an injury, and he will be announcing his decision as soon as he knows what he will do. I'm confident he will make the right choice."

The final wrap-up was an interview with Kiki Mitchell, who explained that even though the face had changed, "the look" was still there. "Annise will never be able to disguise that sensual energy that made her famous." Kiki only hoped that the football player knew what he had.

At that moment the phone rang. Joe ignored it. The answering machine was on. The press was already after him. And he had no answers.

"Joe, this is Lincoln McAllister. I'd like a word with you, if you're listening."

Joe grabbed the phone. "Mac? If this is Mac, I want a word with you, too, you conniving son of a—"

"May I assume you're angry?" Mac interrupted. "So am I. Why did you let her do it?"

Joe swore. "What do you mean? Do what?"

"Let her face those vultures alone. She isn't ready yet. I expected better of you. Why didn't you go with her?"

Joe swallowed another oath and allowed himself to follow the man's train of thought. "I think you're wrong, Mr. McAllister," he said. "My Annie's plenty strong enough to face the press. Didn't you see her? She was magnificent."

The voice on the other end of the phone laughed lightly. "Yes, she was, wasn't she? Why'd you let her get away?"

"According to her, you forbade her to have a relationship with me. She thought she'd failed to redeem me, and she was out of here as fast as she came. But she was wrong. She did just what you wanted her to do. But you know all about that, don't you?"

"Not all. Enough. So, what do you intend to do now?"

"What the hell do I know? If I knew where you were, I'd come and punch you out."

"Tut! Tut! Joe. Use your head, man. I'm not your enemy, you are. Think about it, Joe. Annie was right. Sometimes we have to take a step back to move forward. But you're a life player, you just needed a new game plan." Mac hung up.

If Joe was angry before, now he was a caged bull. What in hell did he mean, take a step back? Even if he did, he still couldn't run, and his arm would never be as strong as it once was. But he couldn't do nothing. Annie wouldn't allow that. Suddenly he didn't want to, either.

Ace understood about that. Ace. Joe wondered how his evening had gone. He'd left with Annie without even checking out with his friend. He could do that much now. He'd seen Annie's concern over Lois. Joe punched in the number.

"Yo, dude," was Ace's way of answering the phone.

"It's Joe. Everything all right there?"

"Everything is cool, man. What happened to you last night?"

"Annie wasn't feeling well. I took her home."

"Lois wanted to call and check on her, but we had to make a little side trip and she had other things on her mind."

"What happened?"

"She almost lost the baby, Joe. They finally stopped it, but it was close, man."

"Ah, Ace, I'm sorry. Is everything okay now?"

"We're both okay," he said softly, "and the baby too. For the first time in a long time, we're okay. I mean it was bad, but it made me see the light, that and you being there for me, Joe. I mean I nearly lost her before I figured it out. Ain't nothing more important than Lois and me."

"I'm glad."

"Hey, Joe, you got anything to do this afternoon?"

Joe laced his answer with ambiguity. "Not sure, why?"

"Thought you might come by the practice field. We're getting ready for the play-offs. It's a long shot, man, but we could get lucky. And I—I need you there. It's not the same without you."

"Yeah, and I could win the lottery," Joe said, then wished he could take the words back. The Falcons had a shot at the play-offs. It wouldn't be the first time a team not predicted to win made a good showing. "I don't know, Ace," he muttered uneasily. "I'll see."

Joe hung up the phone and wandered around the house. Maybe he was just a dumb jock, but he didn't have to be struck by lightning to figure out that he was running out of time.

Annie had only six days, and they'd used up five of them. Wasted days, wasted years, he'd experienced a lifetime of both of them. He'd let himself blame his fear about his future on the loss of his parents and Jack. They had nothing to do with what he was doing now, and it was time he got on with his life.

With Annie.

But how?

He couldn't do anything about his parents, except live up to the expectations they'd had. He might not be able to bring Annie back to him immediately, but he could do something about Jack. He could tell Coach Jones that he'd been responsible for not stopping him from driving the boat. It wouldn't change anything, but it would set the record straight.

It was midafternoon when he crawled into his Jeep and did what he hadn't done in weeks; go to the practice field. When he wandered into the locker room, his teammates all welcomed him as if he'd never been away. He hadn't expected that.

He didn't expect the coach to hug him and tell him that everybody knew that Jack had been bound for destruction. Joe had only delayed the inevitable. "You couldn't have changed that, Joe. If it hadn't been the boat, it would have been something else."

"But why didn't it happen to me instead?"

"You? It's obvious it wasn't your time. Maybe the big guy upstairs had something else in mind for you."

Joe made some inane remark. He didn't want to think about what the coach's words might mean. Everything that had happened since New Year's Eve was taking on some kind of spiritual aura. Though Joe had been brought up on spiritual things, including angels and divine intervention, he'd never taken much stock in them.

Until Annie appeared at his door.

Until he'd learned what it meant to love a beautiful person who was totally committed to a cause—him.

When he left Coach Jones's office he found himself dressing out for practice. "Don't try to do anything more than just simple warm-ups. What I really want you to do is help Ace and the other receivers. I know the man's still got what it takes, but his timing is off. And we need him. Will you do it?"

Joe thought about it for a long time. "I'll give it a try."

Three hours later Joe was exhausted, but he felt like a million dollars. He'd thrown a couple of passes and he'd worked with the team. He might not run the team now, but he could make a damned good backup. After studying the formations for a while, he even spotted a couple of things that might help their chances.

"See, I told you, man," Ace said as they hit the showers. "Sometimes it ain't a player's arm but his heart that a team needs. Why don't you and Annie come over for supper tomorrow night?"

"Annie's gone," Joe said. "Didn't you see her on the news?"

"Yeah, we saw her. We heard her too. She said she hoped you were part of her future. She ain't sure, man. Seems to me you ought to let her know how you feel."

How I feel. How did he feel? He'd thought he was lonely before. He knew now what being alone really meant.

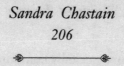

Annie stayed away.

Day six brought a house as quiet and cold as a tomb. The temperature had plunged to freezing the night before and never got any higher. The phone didn't ring. There was no golden-haired angel at his door, and Joe couldn't even eat the steak and potatoes at the Sports Bar and Grill where he'd stopped for dinner.

Never before had he felt so empty. He'd been given a chance at something special and he hadn't had the good sense to hold on to it. None of the news programs mentioned Annie, and the photographer from the tabloid paper had checked out of the hotel and returned to Florida. Even Rob avoided his calls.

After a restless night's sleep, Joe made up his mind that he had to go after her. But nobody knew where she was, and there was no telephone number listed for Lincoln McAllister in the entire United States. After the secretary in Rob's office completed the search and told him the cost, Joe decided he'd have to go back to the team for the rest of the season to pay the bill.

Day seven—Saturday—arrived just as cold and empty as the day before. With the game the next day, there was only a light practice, leaving Joe the rest of the day with nothing to do. He watched game films for a while, then turned his attention to the yard beyond the window.

The birds were pecking the frozen ground. Joe finally remembered that the birdseed he'd bought was still in the Jeep. He unloaded it, and with frozen hands set up and filled his feeders. He opened the sack of feed for the geese and scooped up a bucketful.

He headed down the path toward the lake without recriminations for the first time. He was so intent on his purpose that he almost didn't hear the scream.

It was Annie. He'd recognize that voice anywhere. Where in hell was she?

"Annie! Annie, answer me, dammit!"

His heart was pounding, and he felt as if his lungs would burst. He wasn't there when his parents had died and he hadn't been able to save Jack from death. But this was real.

Plunging down the path, he stumbled on the ice, sliding into a tree, cracking his head against a branch. He heard her scream again. Groggily he shook off the impact and started forward.

He hadn't made it through the patch of woods along the lake before he heard a splash and a low cry of anguish. "Annie?" He pushed through the wet bushes and skidded on the ice as he ran toward the sound. She was standing on the lake bank, one foot in the water, wringing her hands and looking frantically around.

"Don't do it!"

"Don't do what?"

"Jump in."

"I'm not going to jump. Look, Joe. Something is wrong with one of the geese."

He followed the direction of her gaze. One of the birds was flapping its wings frantically. One webbed foot seemed to be caught in the thin layer of ice. The other foot was free and beating on the frozen surface. Overhead, the goose's mate was flying about, screaming in despair.

He let out a sigh of relief. "The water just froze around his foot, trapping him there," Joe explained. "With all that carrying on, he'll break free. Just wait."

But even as the minutes passed and the ice was broken, the bird became even more distraught. It became obvious that the problem was more severe. Joe looked around, trying to see a solution. The goose wasn't more than five feet from the shore, but the water was freezing and this area of the lake was very deep.

He could feel the goose's terror, its frantic attempt to free itself, its waning strength. And suddenly he wasn't seeing the goose any longer, but Jack and the accident. Joe had always thought that he could have saved Jack if he'd only waited to be sure he'd gotten across the lake. But now he wasn't sure.

Seeing the goose struggling brought back his nightmares, the memory of water closing over Jack as clearly as if it were happening now. He'd gone under the dock. It had been dark, and he couldn't breathe. He'd been trapped, just like that bird.

For a moment it was so real that he could even hear Jack's moans, but he couldn't seem to find him in the darkness. He was going to die if he didn't get air.

Jack! He had to save Jack. But he couldn't.

"He's going to die from fright," Annie said. "We have to help him, Joe. Joe!"

"I can't."

Annie glanced at Joe, ashen and still. She gave him a look of dismay, then looked back at the goose. "I can't let that happen, Joe. I'm going to have to get him loose."

When she started to remove her jacket, Joe realized that it might be her under the dark water. She was no witch with magic spells, no angel with heavenly powers sent back to save him from hurling himself off a bridge. She was human, mortal, just like him. And she was about to risk her life for a bird. "Not this time." he told himself. *You couldn't save Jack, but you can save this bird.*

Never before had he felt such sheer terror, such inability to move, such helplessness. It was just like it had been when Jack had hit that dock. He'd been helpless then too.

Now Annie was taking off her shoes. She was about to dive into that same water. He was going to relive the worst moment of his life.

No! Annie was his light in the darkness. He couldn't let her die. Suddenly freed from inertia, Joe peeled off his jacket. "No, just stay put, I'll get him," he said, removing his running shoes as he jumped in. The lacy crust of ice crumbled beneath his feet and the shock of the cold water washed over him. "Damn!"

The cold literally took his breath away for a few seconds. He couldn't move. His chest was being smashed in, so that he couldn't breathe. His head slipped beneath the water, and he had to shake himself to keep moving.

"Joe. I didn't think you could swim."

"I can swim. I could have saved Jack the night he died."

He fought the wave of panic that hit him, trying to focus on the bird, which suddenly grew still, as if it knew that something was about to happen. Instead of pecking Joe to death, it turned deep eyes on him, eyes that seemed to be asking and waiting for an answer.

It's only a bird, Joe. If you don't save him, it won't be like a person drowning. So you don't have anything to lose. Just take it nice and easy. You can do this.

What had seemed to be a short distance suddenly became a marathon swim made in slow motion. His arms and legs turned to weighted steel, and he wasn't certain that he was even moving. He felt as disoriented as he had the night Jack had died. One arm lifted itself as if of its own volition. Then the other.

Never had he been so cold.

Never had he been so afraid.

"You can do it, Joe," a confident voice called out. "Just focus on the light, feel it warming the top of your head and moving down. Feel the light, Joe, the light of pure love. It's on your face now. Your shoulders. Your arms."

And damned if he didn't feel it. In the midst of a lake of ice, he felt as if he were thawing, and suddenly the gander was at his fingertips. He found the foot that was submerged beneath the water. It was caught in a fishing line that was wound tightly around it. The line wouldn't budge. Joe couldn't get a grip on the goose in order to turn him around and tread water at the same time.

"I wish that light had a sharp edge, Annie. I need to cut this line. Otherwise I don't think I can free him."

"You can do it, Joe. Can you move the line?"

He gave an experimental tug. The line was caught in something beneath the water. But with a tug, it could be moved. "Yes, but it won't come loose."

"Just drag it all back to shore. I'll get a knife."

"Sure, I'll just walk back over there hauling a log and a duck through ice water. I'm not Paul Bunyan, darling."

"Yes, you are, Joe. Think Super Bowl. You're fourth down and goal to go. You have to do it. You're strong. You're the one I'm counting on."

And he began to feel stronger. There was no sound of crowds cheering in the background, but he felt Annie's quiet confidence. Joe tried to tug on the line without putting pressure on the now quiet gander.

"Don't peck out my eyes, bird," he said between chattering teeth. "We're going for a little walk."

Meanwhile, overhead, its mate was growing more frantic.

"Tell your lady friend not to lose her feathers. We fellows have to take care of each other." He continued to talk to the gander as he struggled toward the shore.

After what felt like an hour, but was in fact only minutes, he felt the mushy bottom of the lake beneath his feet. Still, there was no climbing up the side. Every attempt he made to get out ended up in his falling back again. The goose was getting alarmed, and Annie's warm light had disappeared from Joe's body.

If Joe let go of the goose, he'd never get another hold on him. The bird might not be affected by subfreezing temperature, but if Joe stayed in the water much longer he'd suffer from hypothermia and they'd both end up as icicles. If he could manage to hoist the goose onto shore, then maybe he could free himself. He reached out and gave a mighty shove, hoisting the goose to the bank. At that moment the goose's mate landed beside her partner.

As if cautioning him to remain still, she nestled beside him and watched as Joe tried unsuccessfully to climb out.

At that point Annie plunged through the brush, brandishing a knife and a blanket. Before attending to the bird, she reached down to Joe. "Take my hand," she said.

And suddenly, as if his feet found purchase, he was able to pull himself up the bank and collapse on the icy terrain, where Annie covered him with the blanket.

Annie turned to the gander and, with soft words of reassurance, attended to the line around his leg. Moments later he was free. Then, as if saying thank you, he gave a garbled cry and, with his mate, waddled to the edge of the woods, where they both watched as Annie tugged at the line.

"I'm going to tie this line to this tree until we can come back and pull it up from whatever it's caught in, Joe," she said, and did it. "Now let's get you to the house before you freeze."

Joe groaned. His feet had no feeling. His body was slowly turning into a chunk of ice. "Sorry, Annie, I can't move. You're the retriever, go get help."

"We don't have that much time. Work with me, Joe. I'm not strong enough to lift you. We have to do this together." She held out her hand again. Painfully, he forced himself to his feet and started toward the house. As he walked along the bank toward the path, he caught a glimpse of a silvery object shimmering in the water and started to laugh.

Annie hurried her stride. He was going into hysterics. "Take it easy, Joe. We'll be inside in a minute."

"No, you don't understand, Annie. It's not that. It was my trophy."

"What was your trophy?" Annie asked as she took the weight of Joe's body across her shoulders.

"My trophy got hung up in the fishing line. Then the goose got caught in the line. There's a lake full of them out there," he said. "I threw those suckers in myself, along with a few plaques, pictures, and assorted other memorabilia."

Annie looked up at Joe. "Why?"

"Because they didn't mean anything anymore."

Annie didn't argue. Joe had just risked his life for an animal. She didn't know what he thought about what he'd done, but she knew that the act of rescue was much more than saving a goose. He'd saved her and himself. All along she'd thought his fear of water was a result of his inability to swim. But the water had become Joe's mantle of guilt and the heavier it became the less important life had become. Without thinking, she reached up and planted a kiss on his cheek. "Thank you, Joe. That was a fine thing you did, rescuing that goose."

"Sure, I'm a knight in shining armor. Just give me a damsel that needs rescuing, and I'm your man."

Annie linked her arm around his waist and set a brisk pace toward the house. "Only one problem, Joe, your damsel was a dude. But it's the results that count."

Joe was soaking wet. His feet were bare. The blanket didn't warm, it simply held the cold against him. But suddenly, from somewhere deep inside, he felt a warm flicker of satisfaction, not to mention a stirring in his groin that had nothing to do with performing good deeds.

Annie had come back. And she'd kissed him. Granted, it had been an impulse, but he felt like a little boy at Christmas. For a moment he remembered the innocence of childhood and the love he'd taken for granted.

At the house Annie shoved him straight up the stairs and into the bathroom. She turned on the shower and let it run. Away from the warmth of her physical presence, he really began to shake. His fingers turned into icy hooks, and he couldn't begin to unbutton his shirt.

"The water's lukewarm," she said, and started to leave. Then, realizing his condition, she turned back and undressed him, removing his sweatshirt, his sweatpants, and his socks, avoiding any conscious attention to his nudity. "Get in," she said.

"Annie, don't go. I need you with me."

"You don't need me, Joe. You never did. I talked to Ace. He says you're back with the team, and he's got his head screwed on right. You're well on your way back to being a productive citizen."

"I'm well on my way to going to jail, probably," he said, his teeth chattering, his skin turning blue.

"I don't know what you're talking about, Joe. Rescuing geese isn't a crime, but turning into an icicle might be. Get in the shower."

He didn't move. "You don't understand, Annie.

I was scared to death out there. I'm still scared. Inside, there's a place so cold that I can't begin to tell you."

Annie took one look at Joe's face and knew he wasn't talking about geese and showers. They'd reached the black moment, the point of no return.

Without a thought she pulled off her clothes and stepped into the shower, pulling Joe with her. He stood, letting the warm water sluice over him, as if he were waiting for some revelation.

"What's wrong, Joe?" Annie said, and put her arms around him, rubbing his back, leaning against his chest. "Please, Joe, tell me what's wrong."

"I don't know if I can. You'll hate me, Annie. Just as I've hated myself."

She moved her hands up his back to his neck, threading her fingertips into his hair, pulling his face down to hers. "I won't hate you, Joe. I love you. God help me, I love you. This wasn't supposed to happen."

"No, and Jack wasn't supposed to die, either. He might not have if I hadn't left him."

"What do you mean, if you hadn't left him?"

His voice dropped and turned to pure steel. "I should have waited until he got across the lake, Annie. I let him die. It was my fault." His arms closed around her, and he leaned down, closing his eyes as he held her, not from fear, but from defeat.

"Your fault, hell. I'll never believe that in a million years. I read the report, Joe. Mac sent it to me. There was a man standing in the marina watching as Jack headed toward the dock. Another boat filled with children cut him off and he swerved to avoid it. That's when he hit."

"Someone was watching?"

"Yes, and he ran straight down to the dock and pulled Jack out just as the boat burst into flames. People came from everywhere. Oh, Joe. All this time you've held yourself responsible for something you couldn't have helped."

"I could have. He'd been drinking. If I'd been driving the boat instead of him, Jack would still be alive."

"And you'd be dead." Annie lifted his chin and forced him to look at her. "Joe, it wasn't the drinking that killed Jack, it was trying to avoid another boat. You couldn't have changed anything. When he hit that dock, it crushed his head. If he'd lived, he'd have been in a coma, brain-dead, a vegetable."

Slowly, he began to hear what she was saying. Slowly he began to let the truth sink in. He'd been carrying that guilt around with him for months, certain that he could have prevented Jack's death or saved him after the crash.

"Oh, Joe, didn't you read the reports, listen to the people who were there?"

"I didn't want any part of all that. I had too much guilt over it."

Finally, as though swimming back through some dark cold fog, Joe looked down at Annie. Her face was etched with concern, caring. "Why'd you come back, Annie?"

"Because I knew you were right all along. It isn't what we do that's important, it's doing it together. I turned my back on a television career, not because I wanted to, but because it was taken from me."

"It wasn't your fault, Annie."

"No, but it came as a welcome relief. I knew all along that I didn't deserve my fame. It was all based on beauty and I could always lose that. What would happen then?"

"You'd find another dream. My mother once told me that when a door is locked, a window is left open."

"I understand that now. But what about you, Joe?"

As he held her in his arms with the water sluicing over them, he felt such a surge of love. With it came sudden understanding. "You were my window open to the world, Annie. There was no crazy man in my past for me to blame my failure on, so I blamed it on me, on losing my folks, on Jack. How dare they die, just when I needed them?

"But they did, and I loaded up with guilt. That guilt grew. It became my stalker. Outside I was still the party animal. I was totally reckless. Nothing mattered. Then, when I began to lose my touch, I knew I was being punished."

"But you earned your fame, Joe. You worked hard for it all your life."

"And I blamed it for the pain in my life. I'd

reached the top, yet I couldn't protect the three people I cared most about."

"And we can't protect each other from bad things either, no matter how much we love each other. You were right. We can only cherish the moment."

Joe thought about the geese down by the lake, touching, preening their feathers, just being together as if nothing had happened.

Like himself and Annie.

He turned off the water and wrapped Annie in his fleece robe. He gathered her in his arms and held her close. "You came back to me, Annie."

"You went back to the team."

"You saved my life, Golden Girl."

"You saved the goose, Joe," she said. She didn't need to explain.

He carried her to the bed, pulled back the cover, and laid her down. "I love you, Annie Calloway," he said, still holding her. "I didn't want to because everybody I loved suffered. I'll try to protect you, Annie. Is that enough?"

"Oh yes, Joe. You've given me what was missing from my life, what I always searched for, only I didn't know it. Love is always enough."

Then they heard it, as clearly as if it were just over their heads. A bell was ringing, light and melodious and clear.

They could never explain it. They never really tried. Because both of them knew the answer.

Somewhere, an angel had earned her wings.

EPILOGUE

A half smile of satisfaction played across Lincoln McAllister's stern lips as he removed the computer disk from his machine, stamped it CLOSED, and slid it into his personal storage files.

Annie Calloway and Joe Armstrong had found each other and, in doing so, filled the dark spaces in their hearts. Sometimes life worked. Sometimes it needed a little help. He stood, walked over to the window, and looked out across the desert, which was flat and cold in the moonlight, like the opaque surface of some frozen lake in the darkness. Behind him the shape of the mountain curled around his house like a hand, protecting him from the world beyond. Shangrila, he called it. Life wasn't perfect, but he continued to work at making it better.

Deep in the earth beneath his rock-hewn fortress, the information of this happy ending would be fed into the computer network that reached around the world.

He let out a deep sigh and, just for a moment, longed for the past and what might have been. But the one life he couldn't change was his own. The darkness was permanent and deep.

Still, there was some solace in knowing that he could reach out through those whose lives he touched, that he could live through others, share their joys and sorrows. And in the end he could make a difference.

The phone rang.

"Lincoln McAllister here."

"Mac, I've got a comatose woman here at Mercy General who won't let herself wake up. There's no reason for her to die, but she seems to have her mind set on it. It's gonna take one of your miracles to bring her back. Any ideas?"

"Mercy General. Hmm. You still have Dr. Nikolai Sandor on staff?"

"Niko? Sure, Niko's an institution here, the devil of the research department. But, Mac, he absolutely refuses to deal with a patient directly."

"A devil or an angel. In my line of work, sometimes it's hard to tell the difference. Niko may be just what your patient needs. What's her name?" Mac asked, and reached for a disk.

"Karen Miller."

Mac entered her name into the files. "Tell me about her."

"She's a librarian. No family, no friends, apparently a real recluse. Best I can tell, the only life she lived was in books."

"So she has no reason to wake up?"

"Maybe not."

"Then Niko will just have to give her one."

"You're sure we're talking about the same man? I don't even think Dr. Sandor has a life outside the hospital. What makes you think he can help Karen."

"Well, maybe one lost soul deserves another."

In the cavern below, lights started to blink and the sounds of computers filled the silence. Suddenly Mac felt a new energy come to life and begin to build.

His smile widened as he pulled up Niko's face on the screen. Yep, Karen Miller needed a reason to live and it was time for Dr. Sandor to come out of hiding. Man. Woman. And desire—the perfect lure.

At that moment a spray of light fanned across the horizon. The sun was planting fingerholds along the edge of the earth as it started up the sky.

A new day was beginning.

Dear Reader,

When I first started this book I had no idea that it would be the beginning of a series based on the presence of angels. In fact, only when my editor asked whether or not the heroine was meant to be a real angel did I consider the question.

My answer was that my angel is whatever the reader needs her to be. There is a certain kind of joy in that thought, which led me to the idea of a series of encounters between angels and mortals who need someone to watch over them.

In the reference books, angels are defined as spiritual beings, guardians, or messengers. They can be either male or female, wise, and sometimes even fun-loving. They may appear in many forms: human, spiritual, animal, or as translucent beams of brilliant light and overwhelming warmth.

I choose to think that each of us has an angel

who cares for us, existing, perhaps, because we need to believe. From that thought came the age-old writer's question—what if? What if there was an actual clearinghouse, a kind of Angels, Inc., whose sole purpose was to seek out those who've lost love?

Lincoln McAllister's Angels, Inc. may be a figment of my imagination, but I'd like to think that it really exists. For now, in the story you've just read, in the stories to come, my angels are as real as my characters and my readers wish them to be.

Now, dear reader, please close your eyes and go with me on a journey to the light. Sense the warmth and listen. Don't you feel them, the gentle brush of angel wings?

Sandra Chastain

Sandra Chastain

"[Sandra Chastain] has a tremendous talent that places her on a pinnacle reserved for special romance writers."
—*Affaire de Coeur*

Sandra Chastain's bestselling western romances shine with her special blend of love and laughter. Now, the award-winning author leads us once again into the heart's untamed territory, where a mismatched couple rides a blazing trail to passion.

THE REDHEAD AND THE PREACHER
On sale in October

McKenzie Kathryn Calhoun didn't mean to rob the bank in Promise, Kansas. But when she accidentally did, she didn't think, she ran. Suddenly the raggedy tomboy the town rejected had the money to make a life for herself . . . if she didn't get caught. But it was just her luck to find herself sitting across the stagecoach from a dangerously handsome, gun-toting preacher who seemed to see through her bravado to the desperate woman beneath.

John Lee Brandon figured that the feisty redhead was running from something. A hired gun, he was masquerading as a new reverend on his way to a mining town called Heaven—and it would take a shrewder lady than Macky to pull the wool over his eyes. But when the town welcomed them as "Preacher Adams" and his wife, he was caught in a charade of respectable wedded bliss. And the two of them were headed for a showdown between lies and love.

Muscle-weary from holding herself erect and trying to keep the money still as the coach bounced, Macky finally gave up and lifted the window curtain. All she could see was open prairie.

No matter how hard she tried to focus on her problems, her thoughts were drawn back to the man who called himself Bran. His boots scraped against the foot of the coach when it hit a bump in the trail. Occasionally his knee touched hers, setting off a fresh tightening of the nerves in her legs.

She decided that her feeling of anticipation was much like that of a moth being drawn to a candle flame. Even though the flame burned, the creature couldn't control its attraction.

In spite of herself she began to wait for the point at which they would touch. If her brother had been there, he'd be taking bets on the next encounter. And, as likely as not, losing.

An unusually deep hole bounced Macky into the air, unfastening her cape and jingling the money inside her velvet purse. Damn banker! Why hadn't all his payroll been in paper money? Why hadn't she left the coins in the portmanteau instead of carrying them on her person?

Don't be silly, Macky, even honest people have coins occasionally. It was just that the sound of those coins seemed to call attention to her, announcing to the world that she was a bank robber.

"Better find a way to stop that jiggling around," the stranger said, in a low, rough voice that gave the impression he didn't talk a lot. "You'll be accosted before you go ten feet outside this coach."

"I have no intention of being robbed," she said, and untied the drawstrings from her waist. No point in trying to conceal what she was carrying. If her traveling companion had been interested in robbing her, he'd already have done so.

Macky tied the coins in the four corners of her handkerchief the way she'd seen her mother do long ago. "But I thank you for your advice," she added in a rare show of proper training that would support her new identity in Denver.

"Wasn't talking about the money," he said, tipping his hat away from his face with one black-gloved finger. His piercing dark eyes came into view, focusing first on her chin, then traveling insolently lower. "Let your loins be girded above."

Macky followed the line of his vision to her chest. The open cape revealed where her blouse gaped between the buttons, exposing bare skin beneath.

"You wall-eyed Peeping Tom!" She swore, promptly forgetting her plan to adopt a new identity, then tugged the front of her dress together. "How dare you quote Bible verse while looking at my—my private person?"

"Wouldn't, normally. Personally, never did have much patience with women that bound themselves up in layers of clothes, but in your case that's a mite safer than opening yourself up to be ogled."

He didn't even try to conceal his amusement. Not many women were so blunt in their speech or so foolish as to threaten a man like him. Any other time he might have reminded her that she was alone and at his mercy.

Instead he reached inside his greatcoat and drew out a small black cigar, then leaned forward to strike a match against the bottom of his boot, taking a long open look at her bodice.

Macky couldn't remember ever having blushed before; she'd never had a reason to do so. But so far as she knew, a man had never seen her breasts before either, certainly never looked at them with such open appreciation. She pulled one side of her cape over the other and retied it.

"I can see how you got the name Eyes That See in Darkness," she snapped. "You're like a hawk, studying the field for his supper."

A moment of fear flashed in her eyes, then was quickly replaced by determination. She refused to be intimidated by anybody—ever again.

Bran recognized that second of panic and regretted that he'd caused it. Whatever she was running away from must have been pretty bad. In a rare moment of kindness he reached back and tried to soften the effect of his words.

"I told you to call me Bran."

"Brand as in cattle brand? Isn't that an odd name for a preacher?"

"Bran, without a *d*, as in devil." A suggestion of a smile wrinkled the corners of his mouth. "You think I'm a preacher?"

"Never knew but two men to carry a Bible around. One was a peddler and one was a preacher. How do you make your living?"

He should never have dropped his guard, but he found himself responding again. "Only answer to the law, a future wife, or St. Peter. We can eliminate the first two and we aren't in heaven yet."

He drew in the smoke and let it out slowly. Macky felt as if he could see straight through her clothing, but she had no intention of letting him know how uncomfortable she was. It came to her that this was a test. If she couldn't stave off one man, how could she hope to find a place for herself in Denver, where she'd heard that women were rare?

"Only thing I'm sure of is that I'm nobody's future wife, certainly not yours."

"Not interested in a man?"

She would have spit if she could. "Nope!"

"Expect to go west alone?"

"I do."

"Full of grit, aren't you?"

"I can take care of myself."

"None of my business," he said wryly, "but next time you put that garment on, turn it around. My guess is that there's more room for your 'private person' with the front of the dress in the front."

She thought back to the woman in the dress shop and the smug smile she'd given Macky when she studied her in the dress. Damn woman. She could have told Macky. But she'd let her go out of the shop looking like the ignorant know-nothing girl she was.

Macky suddenly swung her purse, catching the man's cheek with a heavy whack. Wasn't his fault that she'd reached the end of her control, but he was the one who had caught the brunt of it.

He didn't move when she hit him. Then, like one of those lizards that flicked out his tongue and caught his prey in the blink of an eye, Bran flipped his cigar out the window and jerked her across the seat. He turned her around, folded his arms across her chest, and spread his legs, pulling her bottom close to him.

When he spoke, his voice was tight with fury, not from her attack, but from the unexpected rush of heat that came when he put his arms around her.

"Had a few black eyes in my day, woman, but they

were honest in the getting. Being slapped for telling the truth is something I don't take kindly to."

At that moment the sound of gunfire broke out and a barrage of bullets pelted the carriage door. The driver yelled and the horses began to gallop. The stranger pushed Macky down across the seat where she'd been sitting only moments before, shielding her body with his own.

"The devil's pitchfork! What are you trying to do," she cried, trying to twist out from under him, "smash the breath out of me?"

He curled his arm around her waist and shoved her even farther down until she was in the foot of the carriage with his knee planted against her chest.

"Now shut up," he said, "and stay put unless you want to expose your private person to one of those outlaws shooting at us."

"Outlaws?"

Fear swept over her. Could Pratt have learned where she was? She bit back the curses she'd been about to let fly. The stage lurched drunkenly, throwing her assailant off balance. Righting himself, he drove his leg between Macky and the seat so that he could stand, and jerked the curtain down.

More gunshots followed.

Looking up from where she was wedged between the seats, Macky could see bullet holes in the door. She wished she'd never seen those bank robbers, never taken the money. She could have left it behind in the dress shop. Instead, she'd drawn a gang of outlaws who were trying to kill them.

Instead of returning fire, the driver had to concentrate on keeping the stagecoach under control. The preacher was the only other man around. Macky had the absurd thought that the preacher might do better with a gun than a Bible.

Bran swore and Macky watched in surprise as he drew a gun from beneath his greatcoat. Bouncing around on the floor of the carriage, she was uncomfortably close to her protector. Expensive dusty boots disappeared beneath the fine black trousers covering muscular legs that now straddled her body. He was all man and the most masculine part of him was within touching distance. And given the rutted trail and the horses' speed there was little she could do to avoid touching.

He'd lost his hat, exposing a mass of jet-black hair that curled across his shoulders. Frowning, he slowly raised his head to peer out the window. Quickly he got off one shot, ducked, then lifted himself to fire a second one.

The sound of pounding hooves seemed temporarily diminished.

"Got one," he said, as if he were talking to himself. "Still two of them."

"If you'll let me get up and give me a gun, I'll help."

"I don't have another gun, ma'am, and if I did, I wouldn't let you waste the bullets."

"I'm as good a shot as the next man."

"Don't doubt it." And he didn't. Bran took quick aim and squeezed the trigger. "Now there's one left. Must be the leader—horse has a saddle trimmed with silver."

Macky felt her heart lurch. Silver-trimmed saddle? It was Pratt. She thought he'd been shot. As she listened the sound of the third horse was growing fainter, as if the rider were turning back.

The trouble would have ended there if the wheel

hadn't hit a rut and cracked, careening the coach around and slamming it on its side. Already in a panic, the horses dragged their heavy burden for a short distance, then broke their traces and raced away, leaving the travelers stranded halfway between Promise and Denver.

Inside the carriage the two passengers had no time to brace themselves. When the coach tipped over, it flung Bran backward, slinging Macky against him, her chin slamming his forehead against the door with a star-gathering thud.

When the commotion finally ended, Bran lay still, trying to sort out the situation. Pain shot through his head and he was having trouble focusing his thoughts. He blinked and tried to move, only to discover that he was trapped beneath a heavy weight.

Groggily, he opened his eyes. He was half covered by a very feminine body, which, even in his addled state of mind, had a pulse-raising softness. The loss of her bonnet had freed a mass of wild red hair that tickled his face and clouded his vision. The steady ache of his head didn't stop his awareness of a pair of firm breasts pressed against him. Her chin was resting on his forehead and his left arm was holding her bottom against the part of his body that responded faster than his muddled mind.

Her cape had pulled apart at the neckline and now covered them both like a blanket. As he attempted to lift her he was treated to a view of her blouse, which had fought a gallant, but losing battle. The buttons, now ripped from the shirtwaist, were caught in the folds of his waistcoat, leaving her breasts fully exposed. She was wearing nothing beneath.

Macky tried to scramble up, succeeding only in planting her knee into the body under her.

"Good God, woman, are you trying to emasculate me, too?"

He slid his hand between them and used what strength he had left to help her stand.

"Get your hands off my—what in the name of all that's holy are you doing?"

He let his hand drop. "Trying to survive purgatory!"

"For a preacher, you have a strange inability to distinguish the difference," she said, then bit back her anger as she realized that the man she'd been dressing down was bleeding.

Or rather he had been bleeding, both from his forehead and, from the looks of the panel he was leaning against, the back of his head as well.

"You're hurt," she said. "Were you shot?"

"I think not, but I don't seem to have any feeling in my lower body."

"Oh my. Let me see." She slid one knee between his legs and wedged the other one beside him. She pulled back the greatcoat and looked for blood.

"I don't see any bullet wounds. But you may have broken something," she said curtly, and slid her hand inside his shirt.

Bran could have argued, but the intimacy of her touch shocked him into silence.

"What are you doing?" he finally croaked.

"This may hurt, but we have to know if you broke anything."

His body, numb until that moment, was brought back to life by her touch. When she pulled her hands out of his shirt and began to run them down his legs, he couldn't hold back an oath.

"Here?" she questioned as she moved her hands back up his leg.

"No! I'm all right, I told you."

She moved her fingertips across his groin, prodding and kneading his flesh.

He groaned. Any fear he had that his condition was permanent disappeared as a rush of blood pooled and swelled that part of him that responded to a woman's touch. Unless he stopped her, she'd discover his rapid recovery.

"Stop it, woman! I told you I'm fine. Unless you want me to return the examination, you'll stop fondling my body."

"How dare you, you conceited jackass? I don't know why I was worried that you were hurt. I ought to be concerned with my own . . . condition."

"Let me," he said, sliding out from under her and sitting up, with his back against the floor of the overturned carriage. "I insist."

Amidst a flurry of skirts and tangle of limbs, she managed to stand and back away, ready to protect herself if he attempted to lay a hand on her. "Don't you dare."

"But I do, until I know you're not wounded."

"I hit my head and my stomach feels like it's full of prairie dust," she said quickly, "but I'm not hurt."

"Can you get the door open?"

It was then that Macky realized there were no sounds of life, other than their own breathing inside the coach.

The coach was on its side. She managed to turn around, twisted the handle of the door and pushed against it. It flew open, letting the fading sunlight inside.

Cautiously, she poked her head out of the open door and looked around. Nothing but prairie, and a purple shadow of mountains in the distance.

"I think we're alone," she whispered, the enormity of the truth washing over her like a rush of cold air. "I don't see the driver."

"I think I'll worry about me—us first, beginning with getting up."

But it wasn't as easy as he'd expected. He was still dizzy and his legs were as wobbly as a newborn calf. "Damn! When you said you were trouble, you meant it."

"What does that mean?"

"It means that you have the hardest head in the Kansas Territory."

She felt a twinge in her chin and took in the blood on his face with sudden understanding. "Did I do that to you?"

"You had a hand in it," he said, grabbing the bottom of the window as he tried to lift himself. He thought back to their earlier position and grinned. "Guess that makes us even."

She reached down to assist him, her movement pushing her cape open to reveal her exposed breasts. "Sir!" she gasped. "How could you take advantage of me when I was, when we were—"

"I didn't, though if I hadn't been nearly knocked out by the force of your lovely chin, I might have."

"Get your own self up," she blustered, jerking her hand back and grabbing her cloak to cover herself.

It took her a moment to realize that there was no jingle of coins. She reached beneath her cape. Gone. Not only her purse but her carrying case as well.

"You stole my money," she accused as she watched the stranger grit his teeth and force himself to a standing position.

"You forget, ma'am. I was underneath you." He glanced around the coach. "Your purse is probably somewhere along the trail with my gun, flung out the window when the coach was being dragged by the horses. Horses!" He caught hold of the carriage and looked around. Without horses they could be in big trouble.

His worst fears were realized. There was no sign of any living thing. They were alone. Night was coming and with it the intense cold of the prairie. At least the woman had a warm cape. Still, they couldn't survive long out there. They'd have to face the elements and possibly Indians as well. With the Arapaho and the Pawnee at war there were too many hostile Indians in the area.

He'd spent the best part of his life staying away from innocent, headstrong women. Now here he was, stuck with one who didn't have sense enough to know the difference between the back and the front of a dress, who was worried about her missing purse when they didn't even have a gun.

Bran lifted himself through the open door and slid over the side to the ground, wincing as the jolt set off a fresh round of pain in his head. He touched his head, feeling the sticky evidence of his wound. Apparently his hat had gone the way of his companion's purse.

Macky saw him flinch and felt a twinge of guilt that she'd been responsible for the accident. She scrambled out of the fallen carriage, strode to the back of the coach where Bran was studying the surroundings.

"Everything is lost," she whispered. "Even my travel case—" *The wages of sin.*

"No," Bran corrected her. "It's behind us. I can see something back down the trail where the coach turned over. If I'm lucky, my gun and my hat will be there."

But Macky had already started back toward the patch of color. She could see the wheel, lying where it had rolled to a stop. And something else, a bundle that took shape as she came closer.

"The driver." Macky ran toward the man and dropped to her knees beside him. He was still alive, a bullet through his shoulder. "Are you all right?"

"As all right as a man who's been shot can be," he rasped. "Sorry about what happened, ma'am."

"Can you walk?"

"You're durn right I can," he blustered. "I was just lying here gettin' my strength."

She helped him to his feet and watched as the preacher picked up something, then walked slowly toward her, taking in the driver and studying the landscape around.

"What about your head wound?" she asked as he neared.

"I'll live."

"Unless whoever tried to hold us up comes back. We have a stage, but no horses."

"So we walk."

"A preacher with a Bible, but no gun."

"So, we'll pray."

"I don't have a lot of confidence in that," she said.

"Neither do I," he snapped.

She didn't answer. She didn't really want to believe that the men chasing them were after the stolen money in her travel case. Instead she looked around for the blue velvet drawstring bag and the preacher's hat. They were nowhere to be seen.

"Good shooting back there," the driver said. "Do you see any of the outlaws?"

Bran shaded his eyes and searched again. "No. I

guess the one who got away must have picked them up."

"Who were they?" Macky asked guardedly.

"Probably that gang that held up the bank back in Promise," the driver answered. "The ticket agent told me that one of them was riding a horse with a silver-trimmed saddle."

"Surely it wasn't the same man," Macky said. "There could be more than one saddle like that around." She tried to convince herself that Pratt couldn't have known she was on the stage. Still she couldn't be sure and the thought of being stalked out here in the desert was daunting. "I mean . . ."

She looked up at the two men who were waiting for her to finish her statement. "The sheriff probably caught them," she finished uneasily. She couldn't figure out how they got away.

Bran studied her gravely. She knew more than she was admitting about what had happened back in Promise. Her quick departure was becoming more suspect. Sooner or later he'd do a bit of discreet questioning. For now he'd just watch her.

Watching her was becoming an interesting task since she'd lost that awful-looking bonnet, allowing a riot of rich red hair free across her shoulders. Any thought that she was odd-looking had vanished when he'd seen her hike up her skirt, throw shapely bare legs over the window of the coach and slide to the ground.

Trouble, as he'd begun to think of her, was an intriguing young woman. She had the kind of mouth that made a man lust to taste it at the same time she dared him to try.

He could tell that he was making her uneasy, studying her so seriously. She quickly averted her eyes, turning to the driver, spying the gunbelt strapped to his hips. "You have a pistol. If the thieves return, you can protect us, can't you?"

The driver worked his shoulder and winced. "Not likely, ma'am. They got me in my shooting side." He unsheathed his pistol and handed it to Bran. "You take it, preacher. You're a better shot anyway."

Bran took the weapon, examined it, then inserted it in his own holster. "Ammunition?"

The driver pulled back his jacket to reveal the bullets in the loops of his gunbelt. "Some, enough maybe."

"Good man. At least we're not helpless. I think we'd better get out of here, before the bandit who got away decides to come back. Any idea what he was after?"

"Not unless it was the mail. Ain't carrying nothing else on this part of the run, 'cept you two. Going the other way, sometimes I carry gold from the mines. But they usually send a couple of guards then."

"Look, isn't that the mail sack?" Macky asked, pointing to a bag laying against a rock.

The driver struggled to the bag and tried to lift it, groaned and let it fall back to the ground. "Don't think I can carry it. What about it, Reverend? I'll take your Bible if you'll tote the mail. Can't afford to lose it. That new Pony Express is already getting the mail across country faster than we can."

"How far to the way station?"

"Too far to walk before dark," the driver said. "Maybe we'd better find a place to make camp."

"Make camp?" Macky could sleep on the ground as well as the next one, but she was famished.

Bran studied the driver, then looked down the trail. "Let's get to that outcropping of rocks just ahead," Bran said as he picked up the mail bag. "At least it will give us some protection from the wind." He turned his head, speaking under his breath to Macky. "I don't suppose you have any beans and bacon in that carrying case, do you, Trouble?"

"Afraid not." He didn't have to tell her that she'd have been a lot smarter filling it with food instead of nightgowns and petticoats. "I'd appreciate it if you wouldn't call me that. I had nothing to do with our attack."

"Maybe not," Bran said. "But the name still fits."

"Let me help you, Mr.— What is your name?" Macky asked the driver.

"Jenks Malone," the driver said, pressing his hand against the circle of blood spreading beneath his fingers.

Macky took a step toward the grizzly old man. "You need medical attention before we go anywhere, Mr. Malone."

"Call me Jenks and I can wait," he insisted, through clenched teeth that said how painful the injury really was. "Right now, we gotta find shelter away from the wagon. Cover our trail."

As if on command the wind sprang up, whipping Macky's cape like a sail as she tried to collect it around her. Leaning against the strong current of air, she headed off down the rutted trail, the wind erasing evidence of her footsteps as she walked. Her case was heavy. She was cold and the growls of her stomach sounded more like tigers than termites.

To add to her woes, she faced the worrisome possibility that Pratt might be behind them. At least he was looking for a boy named McKenzie, not an odd-looking woman and a dangerous one-eyed man carrying a mail bag in one hand and a Bible in the other.

THE EDITORS'
CORNER

The business of love has never been as risky or thrilling as in the four LOVESWEPTs coming your way next month. You won't want to miss any one of our heroes' or heroines' breathtaking surrender to desire.

In **THE DAMARON MARK: THE BRIDE**, LOVESWEPT #762, the ever-popular Fayrene Preston offers her most spellbinding romance yet, the first in the fascinating Damaron dynasty. She's a mesmerizing sight in the magnificently lush garden, as perfect as an ice sculpture, but with one soul-scorching kiss, Cale Whitfield can tell she's pure fire. So when the former Secret Service expert is hired to provide security at her wedding, he vows to do whatever it takes to claim the bride as his. Fayrene Preston's talent shines brightly with this intensely passionate story.

Packed with heated emotions, racing pulses, and

seductive moves, Ruth Owen's **BODY HEAT**, LOVESWEPT #763, is one you won't be able to put down. Lyn Tyrell can't believe it when she sees him across the room—Curt Brennermen, her first love, the knight in shining armor who broke her heart and never looked back. Losing her was Curt's only regret, but now the empire-builder with hunter-sharp instincts is being hunted and his beautiful angel is his only hope. Can he show her that only his caress can heal the dark, hurting places in her soul? Find out in this nail-biting tale from the super-talented Ruth Owen.

Charlotte Hughes reminds us what things matter most in **READY-MADE FAMILY**, LOVESWEPT #764. Riley Locke only wants a wife to be a mother to his children, but when Savannah Day arrives on his doorstep he gets that and more! The beautiful spitfire makes him yearn for what he's never had, a lover who can share his bed, his dreams, his life. Savannah follows her instincts and takes the plunge, but once the sparks begin to fly in their marriage of convenience, the two unlikely soulmates must ride out the storm for their chance at everlasting love. This funny, warmhearted romance is another surefire winner from Charlotte Hughes.

Explore the magic of intimate strangers who become kindred spirits in Laura Taylor's **LONESOME TONIGHT**, LOVESWEPT #765. When Michael Cassidy sees Laura Parker rise from the ocean, she's like a vision from his most forbidden dreams, but when she touches him, she touches a soul he doesn't know he still possesses. Fate has robbed Laura of her dreams, but the ruggedly handsome maverick has the key to her secrets, and demands everything she has to give. She's like hot silk in his arms, a fever in his blood, challenging him to realize that true love is worth any risk. A sensuous tale of tough and tender love from award-winning author Laura Taylor.

Happy reading!

With warmest wishes,

Beth de Guzman   Shauna Summers

Beth de Guzman   Shauna Summers

Senior Editor   Associate Editor

P.S. Watch for these thrilling Bantam women's fiction titles coming in November: **BRAZEN** from award-winning mistress of erotic romance Susan Johnson, **THE REDHEAD AND THE PREACHER** from rising star Sandra Chastain, and **THE QUEST,** the spellbinding debut of dazzling new talent Juliana Garnett. Be sure to catch next month's LOVESWEPTs for a preview of these spectacular novels.

 And look for the Bantam women's fiction titles on sale *now:* Following the success of her national bestseller THE LAST BACHELOR comes Betina Krahn's **THE PERFECT MISTRESS**, the story of an exquisite London courtesan determined to make a solid, respectable married life for herself and an openly libertine earl who intends to stay single and free from the hypocrisy of Victorian society. Recognized for her sweeping novels of the American frontier, Rosanne Bittner presents **CHASE THE SUN:** Captain Zack Myers joins the army for one purpose only—to take revenge on the Indians who'd destroyed his world, but Iris Gray longs for the power to tame Zack's hatred before it consumes their love—and even their lives. Finally, Loveswept star Peggy Webb offers her most compelling love story yet: **FROM A DISTANCE** spans the globe from small-town Mississippi to the verdant jungles of Africa with the enthralling tale of one remarkable woman's struggle with forbidden passion and heartbreaking betrayal.

*To enter the sweepstakes outlined below, you must respond by the date specified and
follow all entry instructions published elsewhere in this offer.*

DREAM COME TRUE SWEEPSTAKES

Sweepstakes begins 9/1/94, ends 1/15/96. To qualify for the Early Bird Prize, entry must be received by the date specified elsewhere in this offer. Winners will be selected in random drawings on 2/29/96 by an independent judging organization whose decisions are final. Early Bird winner will be selected in a separate drawing from among all qualifying entries.

Odds of winning determined by total number of entries received. Distribution not to exceed 300 million.

Estimated maximum retail value of prizes: Grand (1) $25,000 (cash alternative $20,000); First (1) $2,000; Second (1) $750; Third (50) $75; Fourth (1,000) $50; Early Bird (1) $5,000. Total prize value: $86,500.

Automobile and travel trailer must be picked up at a local dealer; all other merchandise prizes will be shipped to winners. Awarding of any prize to a minor will require written permission of parent/guardian. If a trip prize is won by a minor, s/he must be accompanied by parent/legal guardian. Trip prizes subject to availability and must be completed within 12 months of date awarded. Blackout dates may apply. Early Bird trip is on a space available basis and does not include port charges, gratuities, optional shore excursions and onboard personal purchases. Prizes are not transferable or redeemable for cash except as specified. No substitution for prizes except as necessary due to unavailability. Travel trailer and/or automobile license and registration fees are winners' responsibility as are any other incidental expenses not specified herein.

Early Bird Prize may not be offered in some presentations of this sweepstakes. Grand through third prize winners will have the option of selecting any prize offered at level won. All prizes will be awarded. Drawing will be held at 204 Center Square Road, Bridgeport, NJ 08014. Winners need not be present. For winners list (available in June, 1996), send a self-addressed, stamped envelope by 1/15/96 to: Dream Come True Winners, P.O. Box 572, Gibbstown, NJ 08027.

THE FOLLOWING APPLIES TO THE SWEEPSTAKES ABOVE:

No purchase necessary. No photocopied or mechanically reproduced entries will be accepted. Not responsible for lost, late, misdirected, damaged, incomplete, illegible, or postage-die mail. Entries become the property of sponsors and will not be returned.

Winner(s) will be notified by mail. Winner(s) may be required to sign and return an affidavit of eligibility/release within 14 days of date on notification or an alternate may be selected. Except where prohibited by law, entry constitutes permission to use of winners' names, hometowns, and likenesses for publicity without additional compensation. Void where prohibited or restricted. All federal, state, provincial, and local laws and regulations apply.

All prize values are in U.S. currency. Presentation of prizes may vary; values at a given prize level will be approximately the same. All taxes are winners' responsibility.

Canadian residents, in order to win, must first correctly answer a time-limited skill testing question administered by mail. Any litigation regarding the conduct and awarding of a prize in this publicity contest by a resident of the province of Quebec may be submitted to the Regie des loteries et courses du Quebec.

Sweepstakes is open to legal residents of the U.S., Canada, and Europe (in those areas where made available) who have received this offer.

Sweepstakes in sponsored by Ventura Associates, 1211 Avenue of the Americas, New York, NY 10036 and presented by independent businesses. Employees of these, their advertising agencies and promotional companies involved in this promotion, and their immediate families, agents, successors, and assignees shall be ineligible to participate in the promotion and shall not be eligible for any prizes covered herein.   SWP 3/95

DON'T MISS THESE FABULOUS
BANTAM WOMEN'S FICTION TITLES

On Sale in September

THE PERFECT MISTRESS
by BETINA KRAHN
National bestselling author of *The Last Bachelor*
"Krahn has a delightful, smart touch." —*Publishers Weekly*

The Perfect Mistress is the perfect new romance from the author of *The Last Bachelor*. The daughter of an exquisite London courtesan, beautiful and candid Gabrielle Le Coeur is determined to make a different life for herself—staid, respectable . . . *married*. Pierce St. James is a libertine viscount who intends to stay single and free of the hypocrisy of Victorian society. For Gabrielle, there is only one way out of the life her mother has planned for her—she must become the virginal "mistress" of London's most notorious rake. ___ 56523-0 $5.99/$7.99

CHASE THE SUN
by ROSANNE BITTNER
Award-winning author of *The Forever Tree*
"Power, passion, tragedy, and triumph are Rosanne Bittner's hallmarks. Again and again, she brings readers to tears." —*Romantic Times*

Rosanne Bittner has captured our hearts with her novels of the American frontier. Passionate and poignant, this captivating epic resonates with the heartbreak and courage of two cultures whose destinies would bring them into conflict again and again as a new nation was formed. ___ 56995-3 $5.99/$7.99

FROM A DISTANCE
by PEGGY WEBB
"Ms. Webb plays on all our heartstrings." —*Romantic Times*

In the tradition of Karen Robards, Peggy Webb offers her most compelling love story yet. From small-town Mississippi to exotic Hawaii to the verdant jungles of Africa, here is the enthralling tale of one remarkable woman's struggle with forbidden passion and heartbreaking betrayal. ___ 56974-0 $5.50/$6.99

Ask for these books at your local bookstore or use this page to order.

Please send me the books I have checked above. I am enclosing $____ (add $2.50 to cover postage and handling). Send check or money order, no cash or C.O.D.'s, please.

Name _____

Address _____

City/State/Zip _____

Send order to: Bantam Books, Dept. FN159, 2451 S. Wolf Rd., Des Plaines, IL 60018
Allow four to six weeks for delivery.
Prices and availability subject to change without notice. FN 159 9/95